PROLOGUE

Amber

Let the record reflect: *Crazy people subject to visions should stay away from crowded airports.*

I roll my suitcase up to the sink in the bathroom and gaze at my face in the mirror as I wash my hands. My hair's still back in a no-nonsense bun, but my piercing headache has turned me into a monster, eyes bloodshot and sunken as if they're receding into my skull to get away from it all.

Great. A screaming migraine on interview day. Just what I've always wanted.

I dry my hands with a paper towel and pat the damp paper against my cheeks, suppressing a groan.

What was I thinking, flying here? Nothing triggers my hallucinations like being around too many people. A guy in a business suit bumped into me, and his memory flashed in my head: him in bed with a woman. He's cheating on his wife.

I don't know how I know, but I do. And I wish I didn't.

Maybe I'll just hide in the bathroom until they call my flight. Yeah, that's a plan. Crazy Amber, hiding in bathrooms because she has visions wherever she goes. I went to law school for this?

My phone beeps. Ten forty-two a.m.. Fifteen minutes until boarding time, and five hours before my interview. I dig for ibuprofen, wincing at the rattle of pills in the bottle.

Let the record reflect: *I need to keep giant bottles of pain meds in my purse at all times.*

"Excuse me." A warm voice sounds behind me, and an old woman touches my back as she reaches past me for a paper towel.

I mean to duck away without eye contact, but the woman has me trapped between the sinks and the paper towels, unable to escape. I glance up with my polite smile pasted in place.

The woman has long white hair but a surprisingly youthful face, and wide blue eyes. "How long have you practiced the intuitive arts?"

I look behind myself, even though I know no one else is there. But the woman couldn't be talking to me, could she? "Excuse me?"

She still touches me, her fingers lightly resting on my sleeve now. "The intuitive arts? How long have you been practicing?"

A chill runs through me. "I'm sorry, I don't know what you're talking about."

The woman's face clouds. "Oh." Her expression clears. "Well, you're supposed to, honey, and you're going to keep having headaches until you do."

My vision blurs with the fast-motion movie reel pictures I've been trying to suppress. Nausea blasts through me. I see a huge, muscle-bound man standing on a beach, brow wrinkled, fists clenched. Then a wolf in a cage, snarling.

I force the breath out of my lungs and draw in fresh oxygen, shaking my head as if that might clear the stupid visions. When my focus returns to the bathroom, I blink. The woman's gone.

Grabbing my suitcase handle, I wheel it out of the bathroom, scanning for the white-haired woman when the clock catches my eye. Ten forty-two a.m. That has to be wrong.

I check my phone just as the two changes to three. Almost no time passed in the bathroom, but there's no sign of the woman.

How did she vanish into thin air?

1

Three Years Later

Amber

I step into the elevator, propping the door open with my foot to hold it for the group approaching.

"Thanks." A deep voice resonates in the small space. A large hand tattooed with the phases of the moon wraps around the door. It's attached to a blue-eyed giant of a man. Underneath his faded T-shirt and tattoos, he's got muscles like Conan the Barbarian. He could probably eat me for lunch and still be hungry.

Two younger men, just as hulking in size, flank him. Shaved heads, a mess of piercings, and more tattoos. I have to stop myself from recoiling.

What are the Hell's Angels doing in my apartment building?

Don't show fear. The first thing I learned in foster care.

Study the threat. Again, foster care, though the lesson carries over to the courtroom nicely.

I draw myself up to my full five foot, three inch height. No matter that I barely come up to the shortest guy's shoulder. I'm a badass, too. Maybe I don't have giant ear gauges or an eyebrow piercing—*ouch, talk about suffering for fashion*—but I'm wearing pointy pumps. They're pinching the hell outta my feet, but with a three inch spike heel, they'll double as a weapon.

"Visiting someone in the building?" My voice has a dubious lilt. I'm not actually a snooty bitch, but when my safety is compromised, the claws come out.

The first guy gazes down at me and the corner of his mouth twitches. "No."

At least this guy looks somewhat normal, except for his huge size. Scratch Conan the Barbarian. This guy is all Thor, right down to his square jawed good looks. I don't normally go for huge and muscled, but damn if he doesn't have my lady parts tingling with new awareness.

I stifle any fantasies about what it would be like to be manhandled by such a guy. And *manhandled*? Seriously? When have I ever wanted to be manhandled?

The three men file onto the elevator, choking the small space. The Three Thugs. Like the Three Stooges, except with more piercings and tattoos. There's so much testosterone in here, it's a wonder I can breathe.

Heat rushes up my inner thighs.

I lean against the wall, hoping these guys aren't up to no good. I don't want to judge, but I wouldn't have survived my childhood if I ignored a threat. And these guys look rough. Their presence makes my skin prickle. Not the stomach-roiling of a full blown vision, but a slight buzzing that can only mean one thing.

Danger.

I stare at Thor's barrel chest, the raised contour of muscle standing out under his T-shirt, and curse my nipples for beading up at such an obvious display of masculine power. What in the hell is wrong with me? I rarely get turned on by men, and my hormones choose this moment to rev into gear? Choose this motorcycle-driving He-Man? He's probably a criminal. I cock a hip and wait for him to explain why they are here.

He says nothing, but one of the younger guys smirks at me.

My hand flutters to my neck, ready to knead away the tension at the base of my skull. I cover the defensive gesture by checking to make sure my updo is secure before pushing the button for the fourth floor. "Which floor?" I ask in my best I-could-kick-your-ass-in-court tone.

"Same as yours," Thor drawls.

Is that a come-on? Or a threat? Are they following me? No, that's silly. They could've just grabbed me in the parking lot if they wanted. I heard their motorcycles roll up, but I never imagined the riders were coming in here.

Thor looks at me, though I refuse to meet his eyes. I hold my briefcase in front of me like a shield until the elevator stops and the doors slide open to my floor.

Please don't let them be after me. Paranoia, my old friend. I'm being skittish here, but the whole reason I'd moved into an apartment building instead of buying a house was to feel safe.

You'll never be safe.

Cell phone at the ready, I wait for the motorcycle gang to get out first. Let's see if they actually have someplace to go. The men saunter off, heading past the door to my apartment and—*oh crap*—they stop at the very next door.

No. *Way.* It couldn't be. "You're my neighbors?" I've lived here a few weeks but haven't met anyone, yet. The new high rise is right downtown, and the rent is pretty high, even for my salary. Not to be rude, but these guys in their ripped-up T-shirts and jeans don't look like they can afford the place. Unless they are drug dealers. Which would be just my luck.

"Is there a problem?" Thor asks.

"Ah...no. Of course not." *Not until you throw a disgustingly loud party complete with biker babes and too much booze.* Frankly, I can't believe they haven't already.

I slide my key into the lock, glancing back to make sure they're really going into their apartment. Thug Number Two —the smirking one— lunges at me, snarling like a ferocious dog.

I shriek and drop my briefcase.

Thug Number Three laughs.

"Knock it off." Thor grabs the scruff of the barking man's shirt and yanks him back. "Get inside. You don't need to scare her." His eyes land on me again. "She's doing a good enough job of that herself."

The two young men stroll inside, still chuckling. I grab my briefcase. Tendrils of hair break free from my hair clip, and I swipe at them to hide my flushed cheeks. Damn punks. My hand shakes, and I hate that most of all. I am no longer the girl who cowers in doorways.

My head feels a little tight, herald of an oncoming vision. I haven't had one in a while, so this one should be a doozy.

Great.

Heart hammering against my ribs, I enter my apartment and start to shut my door. A steel-toed boot jams inside the doorway, stopping me. My eyes fly up to Thor's face, landing on the startling blue eyes. The corners crinkle, and he gives me a predatory half-smile.

I shiver.

"I'm Garrett." He extends his large hand through the gap in the door.

I stare at it for a full two seconds before good manners win out over fear. I transfer the phone to my left hand to take his palm. The heat from his hand envelopes mine, a shock of connection running up my arm. A strange sense of knowing runs through me—like this guy and I are old friends, and I've just forgotten.

I shake off *déjà vu*. Gotta keep Crazy Amber at bay.

"Sorry Trey scared you. I'll make sure it doesn't happen again." His voice is deep and velvet-smooth, matching his rugged good looks. It sends heat curling low in my belly. He appears to be not much older than my twenty-six years. Too old to be dressing and acting like a punk. Although he does it *so well.* Faded T-shirt stretched across giant pecs, tattoos peeking at me from his sleeves and collar. Tousled, just out of bed hair and midday scruff. Mmmm.

Let the record reflect: *Tattooed bad boys make my ovaries sit up and beg.*

I shove my awakening lust back down. This is no time to be turned on. This guy probably mugs little old ladies on his way to motorcycle gang meetings.

"Are—" I clear my throat, trying to sound conversational instead of freaked. "Are all three of you staying there?"

"Yeah. So you'll be safe with us around." He flashes a full smile that takes my breath away. He has deep dimples and remarkably full lips for such a manly man. Chris Hemsworth has nothing on this guy.

Safe. Yeah, right. "Fantastic. I feel better already. Would you mind removing your foot from my door?" I'm going for cool, calm, and collected, but it comes out sounding a little tart.

He gives me a lazy smirk that unfortunately ignites a slow burn between my thighs. "You never told me your name."

"I know." I look pointedly down at his foot.

He tsks, folds his arms, and leans against my doorframe. "Look, princess—"

"Don't call me *princess*."

He raises a brow. "Then, what do I call you?"

"Ms. Drake. Amber Drake."

"You a teacher or something?"

"Lawyer. And you're close to a harassment charge." He's not, actually. They haven't done anything wrong. I don't usually throw my lawyer weight around, but I want to get inside my apartment before I have a vision. Don't need my hot new neighbor knowing I'm crazy.

"We didn't mean to scare you."

"You don't scare me," I say quickly.

"So why are you clutching your pearls? As soon as you saw us, you got your panties all twisted in a knot."

Oh lordy. He's talking about my panties. "I'm not wearing pearls." I use my most lawyerly tone.

"What about panties?"

God help me. The sensitive bits covered by said garment contract at the mention. "No comment." I yank the door, but it doesn't budge.

He raises his hands in surrender. "Figure of speech. You'd be clutching them if you had them. The pearls."

The image of me clutching my panties instead, as he rips them off me with those strong, white teeth, makes my breath hitch. To hide my mounting lust, I go back to scowling, giving up on tugging the door.

"Listen," he says. "My guys are cool. They may look rough, but they're motherfucking Boy Scouts."

I wince at the ill-placed curse word. "Well, Mr....Garrett, maybe you should get back to helping old ladies cross the street." *Or mugging them.* I shoo him, but he doesn't budge.

"I'd rather help you next door to my apartment." He leans closer, and heat rushes over me. It's been a long time since I've been hit on by someone this hot. Maybe never. The lack of subtlety has me rolling my eyes, but I have to admit, there's something to his cocky directness.

No. I am not tempted in the least.

Let the record reflect: *I need to find a nice, normal, non-scary guy and flirt with him.* Never, *ever* entertain the thought of going over to my scary hot neighbor's place wearing nothing but tiny panties and pearls. And maybe a pair of heels.

Oh God.

"Seriously," Garrett's voice drops an octave, the low rumble thrilling me. "Come on over, have a beer. Get to know us."

Can Lawyer Amber turn into Amber the Biker Chick? For a split second, I see myself out of my chic business suit and in tight jeans and a tube top. Hair down around my shoulders, cheeks sun-kissed and tilted into the wind. I cling to Garrett, leaning into the curve of the road as we ride.

I blink. Did I just have a vision? My head pulses a little in answer, but there's no pain.

"So, what will it be, princess?" Garrett's still looking at me, blue eyes friendly. A girl could get lost in that cerulean sea.

Not. Safe.

"No, thank you."

"Okay. Your loss." He withdraws his boot.

My push on the door makes it slam in both our faces. I yelp like an idiot. *Lordy.* I draw in a long, shaky breath. Something has let loose in my belly and somersaults around like a balloon releasing its air.

Locking the deadbolt, I press my ear to the wood and listen. Three seconds pass before I hear footsteps walk away. I sag against the doorway, put a hand to my head. The slight throb is gone.

Let the record reflect: *I need to call building management tomorrow and find out just exactly who those guys are and whether there are any complaints against them.*

For all I know, my apartment might have come available because no one wants to live next to those guys. I sure as hell don't.

At least, that's what I'm telling myself.

"I don't even have pearls," I mutter, toeing off my pumps and setting my briefcase on the table as I speed dial my best friend.

"Hey, girl," she answers. I might be boring and normal—or at least I try to be—but my bestie is cool. Her mom was a hippie, though, which is how she ended up with an outrageous name.

"Hey, Foxfire. How's it going?"

"Trying to keep busy...you know, to keep my mind off it." Foxfire caught her boyfriend cheating the weekend before and kicked him out. About time, but breakups suck, so I've appointed myself her number one cheerleader and activities coordinator until the risk of her caving and asking him back is over.

"Do you want to come to my place? We could watch Netflix and chill." I'm ready for a bit of mind-numbing television tonight. Nothing like silly reality shows to keep my crazy visions at bay. If only it helped my headaches.

"No thanks," Foxfire sighs.

I sense a sad spiral coming on, and scramble. "Hey, you know what we should do?"

"What?"

"Go out dancing tomorrow night. The Morphs are playing at Club Eclipse."

"I don't know. I don't really feel like it."

"Are you kidding me? They're your favorite. You're always telling me how good they are in concert." Most days, I avoid clubs, bars, and any other loud spaces like my sanity depends on it. Which, given my tendency to have visions, it just might. *Foxfire, you'd better appreciate this.* I take a deep breath and lie my face off. "Now I really want to go."

"You? You hate going out. Usually, I'm the one dragging you."

"Uh, yeah, and now I miss it. I know you don't feel like it —that's not the point. The point is to force yourself to get out and be social." I employ the argument she's used on me many a time. "I'll bet a million guys hit on you."

Foxfire snorts. "I doubt it. But I'd love a Cosmo."

"Me, too." It's my turn to sigh.

"So what's with you? You've been working so much lately."

"Yeah, the center's been busy."

"Lots of kids coming through the system?" The gentle sympathy in Foxfire's tone causes my shoulders to unbunch.

"A few."

"Well, I know you're helping them. You almost give lawyers a good name."

"I don't know about that, but helping these kids is necessary. Jesus, so many of them have the most fucked-up lives. They deserve at least one person who cares representing them in the system." I grab a sponge from the sink and wipe down the counter, even though it's already clean. "So...I just met the guys who live next door."

"Oh yeah?" Foxfire drags out her voice in a suggestive tone.

"No, not like that. Scary-looking guys." I recall Garrett's blue eyes and dimpled smile. Maybe he's not that scary. But he definitely left me feeling flustered and off-kilter. "I don't know. I couldn't tell if they were intimidating me or flirting."

"You sound interested."

"No, definitely not." *Total lie.* My hand tingles where Garrett grabbed it. A man like him would be big enough to climb like a jungle gym. Would he let me ride on top? Oh jeez. *Head out of the gutter, Amber!*

I don't want him in my bed. Even though he's probably really good. But good in bed doesn't mean he'll be a good neighbor. Unbidden, the image of me joining one of their all-nighters in my panties and pearls pops into my brain.

Stop it.

"Are they hot?" Leave it to Foxfire to read between the lines.

Even though I'm alone in my apartment, my cheeks grow warm. I let out a strangled chuckle. "Um...yeah. One of them was—is—whatever. But not my type. Definitely not my type."

~.~

Garrett

I lift my palm to my face and inhale the scent still lingering from the pretty blonde human. She wore the hell out of that short fitted skirt and jacket, and as much as she wanted to project prim and proper with her hair up in a librarian hairdo, I smelled her interest. She was aroused. *By me.* And, when we touched hands, I felt the shock of something.

My fingers still tingle from our connection.

I smelled a little fear on her, but mostly the notes were warm and sultry, vanilla, orange and spice. My wolf didn't want to scare her—which is a first. He usually likes throwing his weight around, and feels only impatience for human women. Why would I be interested in a human? And she definitely is all human—I went in close to be sure.

I have no idea why she made my dick so hard. Sassy little thing, pulling her uptown-girl act while her knees shook with fear. I wanted to push her up against the elevator wall, wrap those knocking knees around my waist, and plow the sauciness right out of her. I bet she's never had a proper orgasm. I just might have to show her what it's like to come all over my cock, my name falling from those berry lips like a prayer.

I rearrange my swelling cock in my jeans before plunking down on the leather sofa. Trey and Jared have already opened bottles of beer and stand out on the balcony, talking loudly. Probably not the best for new neighbor relations.

Maybe I'm getting too old to live with my pack brothers. My dad's been telling me for years I needed to take a mate, act like an adult, and make the Tucson pack into something more than an MC club of mostly male shifters. We live loose and free, but the fraternity feel makes most wolves wanting to start a family move to my father's pack in Phoenix, or out of state.

My phone rings, and I check the screen. "Hey, sis," I answer the call.

"Hi, Garrett." She sounds breathless. "Guess where I'm going for spring break?"

"Um...San Diego?"

"Nope."

"Big Sur?"

"Nope, not California."

"Where, kiddo?"

"San Carlos!"

"No." I make my voice deep and forbidding. San Carlos is a Mexican beach town several hours south of Tucson, but, according to the news, is having trouble with drug cartels.

"Garrett, I'm not asking." At twenty-one, my sister, Sedona—named for the beautiful Arizona town where my parents conceived her—is still the coddled baby of the family. She wants full autonomy when she demands it, and full support—financial and otherwise—the rest of the time.

I was ten when Sedona, an "oopsie-baby" was born, so she's more like a daughter than a sister. I sharpen my tone. "Oh, you'd better be asking, or we have a big problem." My folks only allowed Sedona to go to University of Arizona because I live close enough to watch over her. I might be an easygoing guy, but I'm still an alpha. My wolf doesn't tolerate tests of my authority.

"Okay, I'm sorry. I was asking," she capitulates, changing from stubborn to pleading. "Garrett, I *have* to go. All my friends are going. Listen. We're not going to drive through Nogales. We found out there's a safer route. And we'll be in a big group. Besides, I'm not human, remember? Drug gangs can't harm me."

"A bullet to the head would harm anyone."

"I'm not going to get a bullet to the head. I won't be buying drugs, obviously, and I won't be around places where stuff like that goes down. You're being way too overprotective. I'm an adult, in case you've forgotten."

"Don't get sassy."

"Pleeease, Garrett? Pretty please? I *have* to go!"

"Tell me who's going."

A pro at wrapping people around her little finger, Sedona picks up on my crumbling resistance. She plows eagerly into her description of the group. Four boys, five girls, of which two are couples. All human, besides her.

If they were wolves, I'd put my foot down about the mixed genders—not that I'm old-fashioned. With humans, though, no male would be capable of overpowering my sister in any scenario. Still, a spring break beach trip sounds like it would consist of too much drinking and partying, which always results in poor decision-making.

A whoop from the balcony makes me glare at my roommates.

"I want to meet these kids," I tell my sis.

"Garrett, *please!* You will totally embarrass me. That's not fair."

"Then my answer is no."

She huffs into the phone. "Fine. We'll stop by on our way out of town to say goodbye."

Very clever. I'd be the biggest jerk on Earth to pull the plug on her trip at the last minute. My dad would do it, but not me. Which is the main reason Sedona picked a college in my town, versus going to Arizona State.

"Okay. When are you leaving?"

"Tomorrow."

"You're calling to ask permission the night before your trip?" I growl into the phone.

"Well, I was trying to avoid the asking permission thing." Her voice gets small.

"You're lucky you reconsidered." I force my hand to relax. I don't want to break another cellphone.

"So, I can go?"

"You will not allow anyone to drive drunk at any time."

"Right."

"And you will never drink more than two drinks in one night."

"Aw, come on, Garrett, you know I can drink more than that."

"I don't care. I'm giving you my stipulations. If you want to go, you'd better agree to them."

"Okay, okay, I agree. What else?"

"I want a check-in text every day."

"Got it."

I sigh. "Did you get Mexican insurance for the car?"

"Yep. We're all set. I'll see you in the morning. Love you, big bro. You're the best!"

I shake my head, but smile as I hang up. Whoever mates my sister has my pity. It's impossible to deny her anything.

"Hey, boss, you headed to the club tonight?" Trey ambles in from the balcony.

"Not tonight," I examine my phone for cracks. Sedona brings out the protective side of me unlike any other. At least, until I met little Miss Prim 'n Proper next door. For some reason, my wolf has already decided she's under my protection, whether she likes it or not.

"'Cause I was thinking about inviting our new neighbor out. See if she has a wild side."

"No," I growl. My phone crunches in my grip. Rage flares up out of nowhere, surprising the hell outta me. "Leave her alone." Trey's eyes drop to the floor. Beyond him, Jared freezes.

"Just stay away from our neighbor." My wolf is close, making my voice husky.

"Yes, Alpha." Both wolves bow their heads.

Instead of an explanation, another growl rises in my

throat. I'm alpha. I don't have to explain. "And no more drinking on the balcony," I add with a glare. When I open my hand, pieces of my cell phone drop to the couch.

My anger fades as they slink away, but the feeling of satisfaction remains. My wolf is happy we protected Amber. But why? What does one little human matter to me?

Amber

Stacks of files stare up from my desk, but I can't concentrate. Pulling on a strand of my hair, I dial the number for the property manager of my apartment. Maybe I'm being a bitch, but I really think I should follow up on the guys.

"This is Cherise."

"Hi Cherise, Amber Drake calling. I'm in apartment 4F?"

"Of course. Hi, Amber."

"Listen, I'm wondering about the guys in 4G. What's the scoop?"

A pause. "I'm sorry?"

"I met the guys in 4G. They looked really rough. I'm a little nervous about having them as neighbors. Have you had any complaints about them or anything?"

Cherise barks a laugh. "No, I can't say that we have."

"So, they're not partiers or anything? No loud noises or too many motorcycles out front?"

"Do you have a specific complaint?" Cherise's voice turns cold.

Okay, maybe I'm being a suspicious bitch. "No, nothing specific. I just wanted to be sure. You know, they don't look like the most upstanding guys."

"I wouldn't judge a book by its cover." Cherise seems downright annoyed now.

"Right, I'm sorry. I just thought I would check in. You've relieved my mind. Thank you."

Cherise hangs up without a goodbye. Oops. Someone's pissy. But I'm a single woman, looking out for myself. She should understand.

Maybe I was too quick to judge.

I rub my temples. My head throbs, tension radiating from the base of my skull, the way it does when I'm about to enter a bad spell. I felt it coming on from the moment I met those guys in the elevator. My instincts tell me something's up with them.

Unfortunately, my instincts are never wrong.

I drag my palm over the back of my neck, willing the ache away. The nausea is already growing.

Today's gonna suck.

~.~

I CHECK out of work early, stuffing a few files into my giant purse. I probably should call Foxfire to take me home because this headache is affecting my vision. But I prefer to handle my problems solo. I learned as a child never to depend on others or you just wind up disappointed. *I don't need anybody. I can handle this on my own,* is my mantra.

So I creep through traffic, squinting in agony. As soon as I reach the elevator, the migraine hits me. My vision tunnels. My heavy purse hits the floor, and I lean against the wall, finding the button for my floor by feel.

"Are you okay?"

That voice. Even totally out of it with pain, I'd recognize the deep resonant timbre anywhere. God, I'm not up to talking to him right now. Not at all.

It hurts to turn my head to look at him, to focus on his face.

Garrett bends close, peering at me. Concern creases his features. "Amber?"

I sway, and everything goes black.

When my eyes flutter open again, the room spins. No, wait. I'm on the elevator. With Garrett. And I'm in his arms with my head lolling on his shoulder.

He gazes down at me, a little line between his brows. "Are you back with me? I lost you for a moment there. Are you sick?"

I shake my head. Bad move. Closing my eyes, I grunt, "Migraine."

"Gotcha." His chest rumbles under my ear.

The elevator dings, and Garrett carries me out into the hall, striding as if I weigh no more than a feather pillow.

"My purse," I mumble.

"I've got it."

Automatically I relax against him, breathing in his masculine scent. His unshaven jaw brushes against my cheek. Just being in his arms calms the storm of pain raging in me.

By the time we reach my door, I feel almost human again. "Thank you, Mr. ah... Garrett. You can put me down now."

He frowns at the door, still holding me as if in no hurry to put me down. I'm in no hurry, either. For the first time in my life, all the noise in the world, all that distraction I fight to constantly shut out, has faded, leaving only Garrett and me. My hand rests on one granite biceps, feeling the strength in his arms, the controlled power.

I stare at my door, too, wishing it would open itself.

He eases me down and keeps an arm around my waist as I fumble for my keys. Once I have them, I point them towards the door, hoping I've grabbed the right one. I'm still shaky, my body weak from an afternoon spent fighting off the migraine.

Garrett's large hand closes over mine, guiding the key into the lock and turning it. He pushes it open for me.

Quite the gentleman for a guy who looks like a thug.

To my dismay—or maybe delight—he swings me back into his arms and carries me inside.

"Thanks," I tell him, hoping he'll set me back down in the little living room. No such luck.

He carries me straight to the bedroom. I cling to him, wishing I'd stuffed my laundry back into the hamper this morning after upending it all over the floor to find a missing bra. At least the bra is safely hidden under my clothes.

My panties, however, are smack dab in the middle of the floor.

Forget the headache. Now I'm hot all over from blushing. Garrett in my bedroom? I have to admit, it crossed my mind. I never thought it would actually happen.

My room was a lot cleaner in my fantasies.

Garrett sets me on the bed, and bends over me. Before I can say anything, he pulls my pumps off. "Do you take something? Ibuprofen?"

I start to shake my head. *Ouch.* Bad plan. Noise rushes

past my ears. It returned as soon as Garrett put me down. "No, nothing helps but sleep." The nausea makes talking a chore.

Garrett touches me, his huge palm covering my forehead. The agony recedes again. "What can I get you? A glass of water? A wet washcloth?"

Tears prick my eyes, but not from pain. I've never, ever had someone take care of me. "Yes, please," I whisper.

He removes his hand, and I immediately miss it. "Okay. I'll be right back."

I curl up on the bed, leaning into the throb. My skin tingles as Garrett bends over me again. A wet cloth drapes on my forehead. *Heaven.*

A clunk as he sets down a glass of water.

"Do you need anything else?" His brows are drawn down low as his face hovers close.

Who are you, and what did you do with Garrett the Thug? I want to ask. *And what did I do to deserve this kindness?* I know the answer to that: not a damn thing.

"Thanks," I croak. *I'm sorry I judged you.*

"Want me to leave or stay?"

Stay. God, please stay. "I'll be okay. You can go."

He stands.

"Thanks again."

He touches my shoulder. "I'll be next door if you need anything. I have excellent hearing, so just shout if you're going to pass out again."

"Why are you being so nice to me?"

His rugged face splits into a grin. It somehow melts every defense I ever erected against men, in general, and him, specifically. "I intended to hunt you down and give you shit today. Cherise told me all the horrible things you said about me."

Oh God.

The throb in my head intensifies, as if he drove an icepick through my temples. *Killing me with kindness.* "I'm sorry—"

"Nah, don't worry about it. Just rest that head of yours. I'll punish you for it later." He winks. A wink that could bring a girl to her knees.

Not me, of course. But I can see the appeal. Wait, did he just say *punish?* It takes my body a moment to register the threat, but when it does, heat floods between my legs, a welcome diversion from my aching head. I wonder, vaguely, if masturbating would cure a migraine. I'm probably too far gone.

"You sure you're going to be okay?" he asks, and my heart melts a bit more. His fingers stir in my hair, butterfly-light touch brushing back a few fallen tendrils.

Just like that, a vision rushes in. Garrett's face changes, elongates into canine features. A wolf stares at me, white markings around silver eyes.

"Amber?" The wolf image swims away, leaving Garrett's handsome face. Same eye shape as the wolf. His hand rests on my head again, grounding me.

"I'm okay. Please. Just leave." Disappointment rushes through me, but I can't risk him being here while I hallucinate. I want to be nice normal Neighbor Amber. Not Crazy Amber, who mutters strange things while she has her headaches.

What I don't understand is why I feel perfectly comfortable in Garrett's presence, like I finally belong.

I wince as he pulls his hand away. A few seconds later, he closes my bedroom door softly, and I ignore the rush of agony and disappointment, and swallow the words to call him back.

~.~

Garrett

I step into my apartment, closing the door softly, as if the sound of a door snicking shut would disturb my suffering neighbor.

I've never considered myself the caretaking type of guy. I'm an alpha. I growl. I dominate. I demand. But fates, seeing my beautiful neighbor in so much pain nearly gutted me.

I've heard the scent of a wolf's mate's tears will bring him to his knees. Send his aggression level down to zero, unless it's required to defend her. I swear seeing Amber so diminished did that to me.

My wolf chilled way the fuck out, tamping down my restless, lust-driven interest in her and replacing it with the need to soothe away every crease of pain etched in her face. I swear I saw a lifetime's worth of trauma in her young face today. No wonder she's so skittish. I have a feeling she's seen and experienced things a woman so sweet never should have.

I hated leaving her, but what could I do? Set up shop in her apartment when she asked me to leave? I make her nervous enough, as it is.

And I need to lose my interest in this woman, anyway. She's a *human*. Which means, not for me, unless I want a quick fuck.

Oh fates, I totally want a quick fuck.

My wolf growls. He wants more. So much more.

Down, boy. Not gonna happen.

3

Amber

"Look at all the pretty colors," Foxfire cries over the noise of the band. She turns slowly on her barstool before catching herself on our table, doubling over and laughing. Then she makes a swipe for my drink.

"Whoa there, sister." I hold my cosmo out of reach. I've been nursing it since I got here, out of solidarity to my grieving friend. Alcohol this soon after a monster headache episode is a bad idea.

"Sam, I need another one!" Apparently, she thinks she's on a first-name basis with the bartender.

I catch his eye and give a small shake of my head, and he ignores her. "I think it's time we switched to water."

Foxfire pouts and shakes her head before barking with laughter again.

Let the record reflect: *When liquoring up a friend so she can forget her ex, make sure she's eaten first.*

"Maybe we should go outside, get some air," I suggest.

Foxfire isn't listening. She lifts her empty glass and waggles her tongue into it before setting it down with a clunk.

"So thirsty," she whines.

"I'll get us some waters, but you have to stay right here, okay?"

I hop down from the chair to head to the other end of the bar where I can have a private conversation with Sam the bartender about not serving her again tonight. I take my cosmo with me. Foxfire spins slowly in her chair with a drunk, unfocused look. Of the two of us, she's definitely the wild, fun one, but I've never seen her like this before. Maybe she took something when she went to the bathroom. I would've gone with her but this soon after a bad spell I don't like being in close spaces with too many people, and this place is packed.

What was I thinking, coming here? Hunching my shoulders, I weave through the crowd three deep around the bar, trying to make myself less of a target. Too much noise, too many people. One touch too many, and I'll end up in the middle of a vision.

Let the record reflect: *Next girls' night out, I will stick to Netflix and chill.*

A shout goes up, and I whirl. Some girl is making a scene on the dance floor. A few security guys, as big and hulking as my thug neighbors, converge on the scene. More shrieking, and one of the security guys lifts the belligerent drunk.

Crap, it's Foxfire, her multicolored hair flying everywhere.

"Excuse me, excuse me," I push back through pockets of people, no time to keep from touching. Their feelings and thoughts wash over me like the colors of the light show. I arrive at Foxfire's side, lurching like I'm also drunk. Security takes one look at me and hikes a thumb to the door.

"Is she okay?" I straighten, projecting *I'm sober and responsible* vibes as hard as I can. "I just left her for a moment."

"Miss—"

"I just wanna dance!" Foxfire shouts, and windmills her arms.

"Okay." A security guard the size of the Terminator points us towards the back. "Time to go."

"I've got her. I'll get her out of here." I bob next to him, reaching for my friend. I barely come up to his biceps. "Only I'm parked out front and you're taking us to the back—"

I spring back as Foxfire doubles over and starts retching.

"You need to leave," the bouncer says without a flicker of expression. He really does remind me of the Terminator, looming over me. "Both of you."

"Okay, okay, we were just leaving. But I'm parked out front."

"I don't care. You're going out the back door. Now, move it."

Foxfire doubles over again and a second bouncer catches her arm, dragging her forward. "Not in here," he snaps, his double-pierced lip giving him an extra-menacing edge. He reminds me of my thug neighbors. What is with these guys wanting metal all over their faces?

"Hey!" I run beside them. "You need to slow down. She's obviously not feeling well."

The thug bouncer just tows her onward, dragging her when she stumbles.

"Stop," I cry. "You're going to give her bruises. Don't you think getting her a glass of water or helping her to the bathroom would be a bit more in line?"

He propels Foxfire onto the patio in time for her to lean over and puke in a potted plant. "Out," he thunders, pointing to the door to the parking lot.

"Just wait three minutes." I dive to hold back Foxfire's hair. "Back off, or I'll call the cops."

"You're eighty-sixed. You need to get out—"

"Stop." A command ripples through the air. An enormous blond man unfolds himself from one of the patio chairs.

I double take. "Garrett?"

Two strides and my gorgeous new neighbor is at my side, staring Metal Face down. "Leave her alone."

"But she—"

"Enough." Garrett has quiet authority down pat. The guy shuts right up. "Go work the floor."

The Terminator's hands clamp down on the second bouncer's shoulders, pulling him back inside.

"Anything else, boss?" Terminator rumbles. "You need help out here?"

"No, get back inside. I'll take care of them."

I help Foxfire to a chair, digging for the wet wipes I always have stashed in my purse.

"She okay?" Garrett asks.

"She will be."

A cocktail waitress bustles out with a tray of waters. "Garrett? Tank said you'd need these."

"Thanks, Stacy. Make sure no one comes back here, okay? And bring some napkins."

"Sure thing, boss."

"Good girl," Garrett murmurs absently. His eyes are on me.

The waitress flushes and licks her huge, glossy lips, and I feel a surge of hatred.

"You work here?" I ask as soon as she leaves.

"I own the place." He leans against the wall, arms crossed, muscles stretching his black T-shirt. Same jeans, same leather motorcycle boots.

I swallow. "I didn't realize."

"I know you didn't." Same smirk. He's been toying with me. The owner of Eclipse also owns half the downtown real estate, including my apartment building.

My new neighbor is a business owner, not a thug.

"I thought—" I stop. I can't tell him he dresses like a derelict.

Head in hands, Foxfire moans.

"Um, I'm sorry about this," I stand, hands fluttering as if I could conjure away the situation. "We don't usually party this hard."

"One drink is partying hard?"

I blink. "You were watching me?"

He inclines his head *yes*.

"You really should talk to your bartenders. You could be held liable for overserving—"

"Amber." One word stops me. He steps into my space, his body heat washing over me. Instead of feeling intimidated, I relax. *Safe.* "You feeling okay? Last time I saw you—"

"I'm fine," I half turn away, pretending not to be affected, even though every inch of me buzzes, aware, alive.

"You sure about that?" His voice rumbles low, sending a shiver across my skin.

"I'm sure," I whisper. After all, what am I going to tell him? *You touched me, and the visions came, but the pain went away.*

"Here's some napkins," the waitress chirps. Her lips seem extra shiny with gloss. Her gaze flickers over Garrett and I standing close together, and she looks disappointed.

Without thinking, I step into Garrett until my shoulder touches him, as if he's mine, and I have a right to be in the circle of his arms.

A soft chuckle sounds above my head. I tilt my face up, ready to meet his smirk, and, just like that, the hallucination hits me.

My vision blurs. Images flip before my eyes, too fast for me to catch. A movie on fast forward.

I'm back in the elevator, with Garrett and his two friends. This time, I run out to the apartment parking lot. They follow, dropping to all fours, turning into wolves under the giant, glowing eye of the full moon.

"Amber?"

I shake myself, coming to. I'm in Garrett's arms, clinging to his shirt. My entire body flashes hot then cold.

"Werewolf," I breathe, staring into the handsome face that, only seconds before, was a wolf.

Garrett jerks, almost dropping me, and his brow wrinkles. "What did you just say?" There's a sharp menace to his voice and alarm kicks through me.

It's true. He's a werewolf. And he doesn't look happy that I know.

"Nothing." I push away. Beyond him, the clouds part. The moon is full. I need to get out of there. Quick.

"Foxfire, come on." I slip her arm over my shoulder and stand, ignoring her groan.

"Amber, stop," Garrett commands, but I ignore him.

Foxfire and I make it to my car, and, by the time I unload her into the back seat and get her buckled in, my heart has stopped racing. My mind is still running marathons, though. What did I just see? Could it be real? No—that's ridiculous. It was a hallucination. Not real.

"Werewolves don't exist," I mutter.

"Amber."

I leap up with a shriek.

Garrett's standing there, a huge hunk of silent menace in the shadows. "We need to talk."

Prickles race over my skin. In answer, I scramble to my side, slam the door, and squeal the tires outta there. It doesn't matter who Garrett is, or how much real estate he owns, or whether it's true he turns four legged and furry every full moon.

Werewolves may not exist, but the vision made it clear. Garrett is a threat.

~.~

Garrett

As Amber's little hatchback peels outta my parking lot, I touch my tongue to one of my canines to make sure they're still human sized. Little Miss Prim and Proper nearly fainted in my arms—again—then stared at my teeth, the whites of her eyes reflecting the moon.

Werewolves don't exist.

"Fuck," I mutter. My teeth haven't changed. My vision is the same—not domed with the oncoming change. I was on the patio to get some air and space for my wolf, but it wasn't like I was howling. *Werewolf,* she said. How did she guess?

"You okay, boss?" Tank strides across the lot to me.

I straighten, stuffing down my wolf. "Heading home. You okay to lock up?"

"Sure thing. Who was that?" He jerks a chin at the way Amber's car went. "You know her?"

"She's a lawyer. Uptight as fuck. She's also my neighbor."

"Human?"

"You know she is," I say sharply. Tank was one of the few older wolves who followed me from my father's pack. His wolf is huge and dominant, though not more dominant than mine. I suspect he was sent by my father to keep an eye on me, though it's just as likely that, as a consummate bachelor, he prefers my pack to one made up mostly of mated pairs. Quiet, strong, loyal, he makes a great enforcer. One of these days, I'm going to make him my official Second. As soon as I know for sure he's not spying on me for my dad.

"Trey and Jared mentioned a little blonde neighbor. They think you have a thing for her. Said they scented her on you later." He says it like it's casual gossip, but I hear the note of censure, and it pisses me off.

"Worried I'm banging a non-shifter?" Shifters don't usually mate with humans, but that doesn't mean a wolf can't sow his wild oats. There are no laws against it, although more traditional packs—like my dad's—frown on it. I don't. Which is probably why so many bachelor wolves followed me when I left to start my own pack.

"They said you claimed her." Yep. The censorship in Tank's voice is real.

I face him and crack my knuckles. "I told them to stay away, that doesn't mean I mated her. You have a problem here?"

"Dating a human is tricky business. Fucking them is fine, but a real relationship? Quickly becomes a problem. They can't know about us. The rule is—"

"I know the old laws. Have you forgotten who my father is?" I hate invoking my father's authority, but Tank is old school. Some think I wouldn't control my own pack if I didn't have my father backing my rule. It's not true. I've never asked him to back me up on anything, but I guess the threat is there, nonetheless.

"No." Tank drops his gaze. "I don't mean disrespect. I protect the pack."

Authority acknowledged, my wolf backs down. I clap him on the back. The difference between me and my dad is I know when to be a hardass and when to be a friend.

"You and me both. I'll never risk the safety of my wolves over a human. This one is under my protection, but that's all. My wolf took a shine to her." Shit, that sounds even more suspicious. My wolf has no business sniffing around a human. Shifters mate shifters. End of story.

I crack my knuckles again, rubbing my tattoos. Full moon makes me antsy. I'm not a newbie who has to shift, but the desire is there.

"I'm heading out. Tell Trey and Jared no after-work party, or they'll be on dish duty for a month."

"Right, boss." Tank tilts his head, showing his neck a little in deference. He doesn't argue, or point out that my explanation of who Amber is and what she means to me falls short. Wolf packs aren't democracies. My word is law. All the more reason not to be an asshole like my father.

But Tank was right to give his warning. We all know the rules. Outsiders can't know about us. In the old days, there was only one way to deal with a human who'd learned the shifter secret.

If Amber knows what I think she knows, she might have to die.

~.~

A LONG, winding ride does nothing to calm my wolf. All too soon, I find myself striding down the hall of my apartment building straight to Amber's door.

My phone buzzes, and I pull it out. There's a text from my sister with lots of happy face and palm tree emojis. *Arrived in San Carlos. XXOO.*

I shake my head, fight a grin as I refocus on the matter at hand.

An outsider knows our secret. My wolf doesn't think of her as an outsider, though. He wants to protect her as much as I want to protect my sister.

Leaning close to the door, my skin tingles as I pick up Amber's sultry scent. Inside, a TV is on low, and I hear her moving around. Amber must have dropped off her friend and come back here. There's no other scent.

I knock on the door. The apartment falls quiet.

"Amber."

More silence.

"I know you're in there. It's Garrett. I need to talk to you."

Her scent grows stronger. There's a slight rustle just behind the door. I realize I'm gripping the doorknob and pull my hand away. I don't need to crush another thing this month.

"Open up." I lower my voice. She's right there, on the other side.

She doesn't answer.

I throw some authority into my voice. "Amber, open the door."

"I'm busy."

"Open it. *Now.*"

"Go away. Or I'll call the cops."

"No." I splay my hand on the door, as if I can feel her through the wood. "Calling the cops would seriously piss me off, and believe me, little girl, you don't want to see me mad." *True story:* I don't want her to see me mad. "Now, open the door."

"Go to hell. I'm not afraid of you."

The corners of my lips tug upward, despite the seriousness of the situation. I love her bravado. She's so fucking cute. "Right. So, if you're not afraid, *open the door.*" When she doesn't answer, I ball my hand into a fist. "Open it, or I'll bust it in, Amber."

"I'm calling the cops."

"*No cops.* Door. Now." I'm not used to being disobeyed—by my wolves or by humans. Usually, when I show my authority, people jump.

She moves away. Is she calling the cops?

Fuck. I'm so used to people following my orders, I didn't think she'd actually go through with her threat. I angle my ear to the door but don't hear her speaking. Instead...*dammit.* That's the sound of her balcony door snicking open. Where is she going?

The image of her attempting the crazy and dangerous gymnastic feat of leaping to the neighboring balcony to escape throws me into full shifter protection mode. My fangs punch out to defend her from the invisible enemy of gravity. I race back to my apartment and run out to the balcony.

Fuckity fuck fuck!

The crazy little human has climbed over the edge of her balcony and is inching her way to the fire escape ladder.

I swallow the shout that chokes my throat, not wanting to scare her. She's obviously already terrified if she thinks climbing off her balcony is a better option than facing me. But, yeah, I guess finding out your neighbor is a werewolf would scare the shit out of most humans.

I dash to the stairwell and take each landing in one leap, skipping the stairs altogether. On the first floor, I bang the door open and jog around to the back of the building. Adrenaline pulses through me, bringing on a partial shift. My skin ripples before I take a deep breath and settle. My night vision sharpens.

There. Amber, still in her little skirt and blouse from the club, her hair in her usual bun. She's climbing down the metal rungs of the fire escape, barefoot. Her foot slips a little, and she yelps, clinging to the railing. She's going too fast.

I race over just as she loses her footing again and slips. With a little scream, she falls the rest of the way—about a story and a half—right into my arms. I catch her easily but soften my body to cushion her landing, letting her knock me to the ground. A grunt escapes as I hit the cement. For a second, I just lie there, cock growing hard at the feel of her in my arms.

She's breathing, heart racing. Her scent, sweet citrus and spice, makes me dizzy. I rest a hand on her back, encouraging her to lie still, her breasts pressed against my chest. Maybe she'll take the hint and relax into me.

No such luck. She pushes up, straddling me as she stares down.

Oh, honey. Not a good idea.

My cock thinks it's a fabulous idea. It strains against my jeans, wanting more contact. "That was a stupid-ass move."

She scrambles up, but I catch her, coming to my feet to swing her over my shoulder. I'm halfway to the stairwell when she starts to struggle.

"Put me down, Garrett! I will scream."

Interesting she hasn't already screamed. Just like she didn't call the cops. Maybe she obeys better than I thought.

Either way, I have the upper hand, and I intend to keep it.

I hoist her higher on my shoulder, cutting off her protests. I give her bottom a slap, which is a big mistake. It's got to be the cutest ass I've ever seen, and now that I've smacked it once, I'm dying for more contact. I want to squeeze it, stroke it, smack it again.

She sucks in a breath. I scent feminine arousal.

Oh, honey, it's on.

I carry her in through the back door, taking the steps two at a time. I blow past her apartment and slide the key into my lock, kicking open the door.

As I carry her inside, she starts struggling again. I shut the door and stride to the couch, where I plop down and pull her over my knee. Now that the idea's in my head, I can't let it go.

"Never, ever run from a wolf." I deliver three hard slaps to her tight little ass. How I keep from squeezing it when I'm done, I'm not sure.

"Ow," she yelps and kicks. "Knock it off."

Her wriggling only turns me on more. I can't resist three more spanks, just as hard. The scent of her arousal fills the room. The need to fuck hits me so hard, I have to pause with my hand splayed over her ass. And she waits, silent, draped over my knees like the good little submissive she is.

Got your number, princess.

I shove the short skirt up and nearly groan at the sight of her panties. Fucking pink satin. With tiny black bows at the bottom of each cheek. The curves beneath the fabric blush with my handprints. My wolf howls with satisfaction. "Oh that's pretty, baby," I murmur.

She starts to wriggle again, so I pick up spanking, slapping her panty-clad ass with slow, deliberate strokes.

"You never run from a wolf because it triggers our hunting instinct. You don't want to be caught by the animal, baby. Not a delicate little human like you."

She lets out a wanton moan and rolls her hips to and fro as I spank her pert little ass. Her hip rubs over my aching cock, torturing me with every small movement.

I pull her panties up into her crack, baring more of her cute ass. Her cheeks are already rosy from the punishment I've laid down, but, now that I've started, I'm in no mood to stop. Not when it feels so good to master her. Not when she loves to hate it. I can tell because the sweet nectar of her arousal fills the room, driving my wolf mad with desire.

I slap her bare cheeks, the sound laying down the beat for her vocalizations—the cutest little cries and grunts.

Only when one cry sounds a little too much like a sob do I stop.

Shit.

Did I go too far? Wolves are physical creatures. We're swift to issue consequences—usually physical. Females get spanked by their mates. But she's not one of us.

I rub her reddened cheeks, lift her up, and sit her on my lap. Her curves fit perfectly. "And do not let me catch you endangering your life like that again. You scared the crap out of me."

"*I* scared *you*?"

Her little skirt is up to her waist, bare thigh and panties filling my eyes. My cock aches, and I bite back the growl rising in my throat.

"Let go of me." She writhes as if she wants to get up, but when I lock my arms around her, excitement blooms in her scent.

My good girl likes being restrained.

I've never been with a human who likes rough play.

Bedding humans is allowed—as long as we don't let slip who we are. But humans don't usually interest me. Too weak, delicate.

Not this little she devil. If she doesn't stop fighting me, I will pin her face down on the floor and take her hard from behind, make her scream for a different reason. A far better reason.

But I have the feeling fucking her wouldn't get her out of my system. Whoever this female is, she means something more to my wolf.

"Do you know what I do for a living?" she grinds out, still squirming. "I'm an attorney, and I will sue your sorry—"

"You're not going to sue me," I drawl.

"I will notify the police and file a restraining order and—"

~.~

Amber

"Shh," my neighbor—my *werewolf* neighbor—soothes. He runs his hand over my bare thigh. I go still. Part of me wants to rip his eyes out, but the other part of me holds its breath, trembling under his caress, waiting to see what he'll do next.

"You're not going to call the cops, and you're not going to file a lawsuit." He is annoyingly certain.

My bottom stings and tingles from the smacks he delivered but my pussy is molten. What the hell is wrong with me?

"You don't want to get into a battle of wills with me, because you won't win."

"Is that a threat?"

He chuckles, his hand slipping around the curve of my knee and sliding up my inner thigh. "No. It's a fact."

His arm hooks around my waist, pulling me close as I straddle his knee. His big hard thigh presses against my pussy. I rock down on it and let out a puff of air then immediately stiffen.

"You are so..." His eyes rove over me, lingering at the line of my cleavage. Damn this bra. "Cute."

I will sue you, buddy. Sexual harassment. Infringement of tenant rights. A litany of law marches through my head, but his next words scramble every thought in my brain.

"And naughty." He kneads my ass, still bare due to the wicked wedgie he gave me. A wonderful wedgie that also stimulates my clit. I rock my pelvis over his thigh, grinding down to stimulate the little nubbin.

Garrett barks out a curse, and his hands tighten on my ass. His eyes look more silver than blue. He flips me around to face away from him, as if I weigh nothing. My knees drape over his thighs, spread wide.

"You need relief, baby?" His voice is thick and growly. His fingers zero in on the exact place I need them, rubbing my clit over the satin of my panties. Garrett's other hand cups my breast, kneading and squeezing. My nipples pucker under my bra, breasts ache and pulse in time with my clit, which he circles with the pad of a finger. "I need you to answer me."

"Y-yes." Panting, I reach down and yank the gusset of my panties aside for him.

Garrett groans. "Oh yeah, baby. That's it. Offer that sweet little pussy to me."

His digits are huge. They glide over my slit, which is embarrassingly wet. I tip my pelvis down to meet his touch, urge him on. He works his middle finger inside me.

It's been forever since I've had sex, and I'm sure it shows because I'm almost orgasming the second his digit pumps inside me. I don't recognize the sounds coming from my throat.

Garrett adds a second finger, stretching me.

I throw my head back on his shoulder, crying out with pleasure.

He thrusts them in and out, uses the heel of his hand against my clit until I'm nearly weeping with desire. When he abruptly pulls them out, my pussy clutches on emptiness. He delivers a sharp slap, right between my legs. "Naughty girl," he growls in my ear.

My hips jack up.

He spanks my pussy again. A third time. Then, like he knows I'm about to blow, he shoves two fingers inside me and fucks me hard and rough, not holding back, delivering the intensity and speed I need to crest the peak.

I shriek and throw my head back on his shoulder, digging my nails into his forearms as I ride his digits, my hips bucking, pussy clenching, toes curling. My orgasm goes on and on while Garrett holds his fingers wedged inside me and I come all over them.

God help me. I've never lost control like that. Never allowed anyone to give me so much pleasure or to see me out of my mind.

He eases them out as I coast down the other side, my body going limp against his. His lips find my shoulder and he smooths my panties back in place. "That's it, naughty girl," he murmurs in my ear, then rearranges me to face him once more.

He brushes a strand of hair back from my face. "My naughty little human." He emphasizes the last word, looking me in the eye, and it all comes rushing back. He's a werewolf, and *he knows I know.*

I tense. What's he going to do?

But werewolves don't exist. I must have been off my rocker. "I'm not crazy," I blurt.

His stern look softens a fraction. "I never said you were."

"Are you...you're not—"

He arches a brow. "Not what?"

"Werewolves don't exist," I repeat my assertion from earlier, but my gaze falls to his tattooed knuckles. The phases of the moon.

Oh God. He's definitely a werewolf.

I try to bolt again, but he holds me easily, his arm like a steel band around my waist.

"Wh—" I clear my throat. "What are you going to do with me?"

"I don't know. First I need you to answer some questions for me." He sounds serious now.

"Like what?"

He shifts me to the side. Taking my hands, he turns them over, examining my arms. "Are you hurt at all, baby?"

Biting back tears, I shake my head. There he goes, taking care of me again.

"Good." He lifts me from his knee and sits me on the coffee table in front of him, holding both my hands in one of his big paws. The intensity of his gaze makes me blush again. At last, he asks, "How did you know?"

I try to jerk my hands free, but he holds me fast, adding his other hand almost like he's comforting me, rather than holding me captive. I pull harder.

"Hey," he says. "Settle down. I'm not going to hurt you, but I do need you to answer me."

"There is no answer," I rasp. I don't talk about my

visions, ever. Last time I did, I was thirteen, and it cost me my foster home. I learned quickly that people don't like having their secrets spilled for them. I don't know how I let my knowing slip this time.

Garrett just waits, holding me without effort, saying nothing.

I slump. He's not going to let me go until I tell him. "Sometimes I just know things," I mumble. "I see them, like fast-forward pictures."

"What do you mean?"

I stare at a hole in his jeans, wishing I had just stayed at Foxfire's place. Sent a moving company to get my stuff, found a way to avoid Garrett for the rest of my life.

But I didn't. Because, deep down, I wanted to see him. Needed to know if the vision was true.

"Amber?"

I shrug. "I don't know. I really don't. Sometimes I see stuff I wish I hadn't. Like dead people or the future—usually something bad, like accidents or deaths." I remember asking my foster mom why the two buildings in New York caught fire and fell—two months before the 9/11 attacks. That family returned me in a hurry after it came true. "I don't do it on purpose. I hate it, actually."

"You're psychic."

I jerk my hand out of his and swipe at my face. My hair's fallen out of my updo. I probably look a mess. Crazy Amber, the psychic. All I need is to carry a deck of Tarot cards, wear flowy skirts, and cover my apartment with crystals. Oh, and burn incense. Then I can hang up a shingle and tell fortunes.

Garrett's watching me, stone cold serious. I swallow hard. I know he's a werewolf. Probably something he doesn't want getting out.

My fear from earlier returns: I might die tonight. But no, if he wanted me to die, he would've let me fall off the balcony. Unless he needed to question me first.

"Did you tell your friend?"

Right. This is what he needed to know. "Foxfire? No. She passed out on the way home."

"Are you going to tell her?"

"No." My voice cracks. "No way. I'm not going to tell anyone. I don't need people thinking I'm crazy." *Knowing I'm crazy.*

"Are you just saying what I want to hear?"

"Do I seem like the sort of woman to blow smoke up your butt?"

He grins, a devastating smile that makes my insides quiver. "You did say you're an attorney." He drops his huge palms onto my knees. I stare at the tattooed knuckles, the large fingers caressing me. I never knew legs could be so erotic. I'm still dizzy from my last orgasm, but I wouldn't be opposed to round two.

"Would you give me your word?"

I nod once then several more times. Is that really all he wants? A promise I won't talk?

He squeezes my knees. "Thank you. Listen, I don't want to threaten you...but wolves don't like humans to know about us."

"Well, I didn't exactly ask to know."

He crooks that smile at me again, making my limbs turn liquid. "I know that, Amber. I just want you to understand that you and I are going to have big problems if you talk."

"You'll spank me again?" Damn, I was supposed to sound annoyed, not breathy and fluttery. As if I want to be bare-assed over his lap again. Oh wait. I totally do.

"Did you like your spanking, Amber?" His voice rumbles, deep and seductive.

"No." I want to stand up, but he's leaning forward, rough palms on my thighs, and I would have to push him away. Touching him would be dangerous.

"I think you did." Sexy wrinkles appear in the corner of his eyes. He's laughing at me.

"If I told someone you were a werewolf, what would you do to me?" I ask, mostly to kill the mood.

His blue eyes turn to ice chips. His hands squeeze my knees, and I wonder that I ever thought his touch sexy. My body freezes, as I stare down a predator.

"You don't want to know," he rumbles, totally serious. The threat in his eye effectively kills the sexy mood.

"All right, then." I find my voice somehow. "I don't need to know. I won't tell anyone, on the pain of death." I try to say that last part like it's a little joke but fumble it. My stomach feels like a bottomless pit.

His big body relaxes. After a moment, so does mine.

"Good girl," he says.

A sigh escapes me, so big it rattles my bones.

"Come here," he murmurs, and gathers me in his arms. I stay stiff, stunned, before melting against him.

"I'm sorry if I scared you tonight." His voice reverberates in his big chest. His hand soothes up and down my back. It feels so damn good.

"Oh, I wasn't scared. I normally climb down from my balcony at two in the morning."

His chuckle warms me. "I really like you, Amber." He stands and sets me on my feet, as if he hasn't turned my world upside down. "I hope we have an understanding?"

"Yeah. My lips are sealed."

"Good girl."

Fuck. Those words.

I raise my chin. "I'm reserving the right to sue you for assault and battery."

He grins again. A toothy, wolfish grin that makes my pussy clench. He reaches down and tucks a strand of hair behind my ear. "I would apologize," he purrs. "Except I'm not sorry at all. I enjoyed seeing that gorgeous little ass of yours. And those panties—" He makes a satisfied, growly sound. Yep, another clench. "Come on, baby. It's late, and you should get some rest." He leads me out, a palm on my back. I thought he might just close his door behind me, but he escorts me to my apartment like a gentleman. We stand in front of the door a second before I remember.

"Crap. It's locked."

"I'll get it. I'm good with locks."

He disappears back into his apartment and re-emerges with a wrench and another small tool.

"You're going to pick my lock?"

"It's a good skill to have, not that I use it much. I'm more of a huff and puff and blow your door down kinda guy."

A half-hysterical laugh bubbles out of my throat. "You don't keep a master key to all the apartments? Wouldn't that be easier?"

"This is more fun. Wanna learn how? I'll teach you. It's actually pretty easy. Come on," he says when I hesitate. "Unless the princess is too good to get her hands dirty."

"No," I scoff.

"This is what happens when you hang with a bad boy." He winks, and gives me the wrench.

He talks me through breaking and entering while slouching against the wall. "Okay, so the tension wrench goes into the bottom of the key hole. No—" His large hand swallows mine, and I jerk.

"Easy," he murmurs in my ear, and suddenly there's no air to breathe. He shifts the wrench, showing me how to apply tension in the direction my key would normally turn. "Now, you insert the pick at the top. Yes, that's it. Move the pick back and forth in the keyhole to lift each pin. Whoops —you released the wrench. You have to keep applying pressure there, because that's what will actually open the lock. Try again."

Let the record reflect: *Picking a lock is easy.* Or, it would be, if I weren't pressed up against a giant hottie. Electricity runs through my body, tiny shocks pulsing between my legs. My head swims with Garrett's deep voice and patient instruction. He's so gentle, yet he carried me like a war prize just a few minutes before. Carried me in and spanked me. *Oh God.* Every time I think of it, my belly gets fluttery, and my pussy clenches. And even when he threatened me, I felt safe.

My shaking fingers slip. "I can't do it."

"Sure you can. Try again. It's easy once you have the hang of it. Slow and steady, Counselor," he murmurs as I jiggle the pick back and forth.

One by one, I release the pins, and the wrench turns. "I did it!"

He grins as he opens the door for me. I try to give the tools back to him, but he waves them away. "Keep them. They might come in handy."

"You're my landlord. Should you be encouraging all this breaking and entering?"

"I trust you to be good." He puts a finger under my chin and lifts my face to his. His handsome face fills my vision. "Until I make you bad."

I can't breathe. Is he going to kiss me?

He drops his finger. "Remember what we talked about."

"Or else?" His closeness emboldens me. I'm giddy. Or maybe I've just lost my mind.

"Or else." His eyes are flint, striking sparks. "You'll be punished."

I lick my lips. "What do I get if I'm good?"

A pause then he crowds me against the door. Two giant hands come to cup my face, tilting it up before his lips slam down on mine.

It's a great kiss. A bad boy kiss. A naughty girl kiss. He pins me against the door, mouth dominating mine. His knee presses between my splayed legs, his hard thigh angling against my pussy. Sparks fly in my mind, my body reigniting like fireworks on the Fourth of July. I grind down, helpless against the rising tide.

Let the record reflect: *Werewolves kiss good.*

At the last moment, he breaks away.

"Damn," I breathe.

"That's right, baby." He angles his hips, and his erection brushes against me. "Be good, and you just might get another reward."

~.~

Garrett

I sit sipping beer on my couch, staring at the moon as I try to get my wolf under control. Bad, bad girl, running from a wolf. And the way she responded to the spanking... damn if my dick isn't all awake and ready to go.

I hear boots in the hall before my apartment door bangs open.

"Not so loud," I call, and wince. I sound like my dad.

Why the hell did I think it was a good idea to live with packmates? It was fun just out of college, but I'm twenty-nine, and a business owner. I own half the real estate downtown. Maybe it's time to buy a house, find a mate. Grow the fuck up. But that would make me into my dad.

Damn, my wolf is riled up if I'm thinking about mating.

Trey and Jared stride inside only to stop short.

"What the—" Trey starts, his eyes turning silver.

"It's cool," I tell them. They smell Amber.

"What's with you and the human? Tank said you took off after her," Jared says.

I scoff. That makes me sound desperate. "Tank was wrong. I went for a ride then came back here. You know, the place where I live."

Jared's eyes aren't silver, but he raises his head, sniffing like a wolf at Amber's lingering vanilla scent. "But she was here."

"She and I had a little talk." I take a pull on my beer, keep my tone casual. "She knows."

Jared and Trey go still.

"How?" Trey asks. His shoulders bunch like he's about to change. Jared sits down on a chair facing me. A string of tension runs through him, too, like a predator on high alert.

And they're right to prepare to defend. Amber knowing is a liability to the pack.

"Back off." I can't quite keep the growl out of my voice. "She's one of us."

"What?" Jared cocks his head.

"You told her?" Trey asks as if he didn't hear me, worrying his lip piercing with his tongue. He's the thinker of the pack. I should have forced him to go to college because he's the guy who researches the fuck out of anything and everything that interests him. He's a great advisor and strategist. "Humans can't know about us, G. The rule—"

"Shut up, Trey," Jared cuts him off. It's inappropriate for either of them to question any decision I make.

I plunk my beer down. "No, I didn't tell her. And I'm aware of pack rules. That particular one hasn't been enforced for seventy years."

"Yeah, because your dad would rip a shifter's guts out if they ever told a human," Jared mumbles. His eyes are silver, too.

"I'm not my father." The guys freeze at my growl, so I force myself to relax. "That might be how my dad runs things, but I don't think it's necessary. Like I said, she's one of us."

"Shifter?" Jared asks, though he must already know by her scent she's not.

I shake my head. "Psychic. I didn't tell her. She guessed. Or knew." I stand and cross my arms over my chest. "But, we talked, and she's not going to say a word."

Trey gnaws his lip.

Jared watches me. "You gonna tell Tank?"

My fingers curl into fists. Is Tank their fucking leader now? "No need. She's not gonna breathe a word."

"Whenever you talk about her, your wolf is in your eyes," Jared observes. "We've been taking bets on how long before you claim her."

They've been taking bets. Which probably means the whole pack knows I have a thing for a human. Assholes.

"I want to protect her," I admit. *And fuck her senseless.* "She's a good person, and she doesn't mean to have these visions." And my wolf wants her safe. At first I was going to deny the truth, but for some reason didn't want to lie to her.

I'm not crazy, she said, and it was all over. I couldn't let her go on thinking that. I couldn't hurt her. I'm an alpha. I protect the weak. Whoever Amber Drake is, she's one of mine.

"She's one of us," I repeat. "She swore not to tell, and I believe her. And my wolf trusts her, so..." I shrug, watching their body language carefully. Most of my pack is loyal, but I'm bending the rules. One hint of them being a threat to Amber, and I'll do what I must to make sure she's safe.

"Whatever you say, boss." Trey drops into a seat next to Jared.

I grunt my approval, but, secretly, I'm glad they're taking this so well.

"Yeah," Jared also lounges back, relaxed and smiling. "It's about time you took a mate."

My eyes almost bug out. "What?"

"We followed you to Tucson because your dad's pack was too rigid. No room for a wolf to run. But all this bachelorhood is wearing on us. I'm ready to chase down a little she-wolf, give her a claiming bite. I think a lot of guys are, but we've been waiting for you."

"Bullshit." These guys are party boys. The idea of any of us settling down anytime soon is ludicrous.

Jared just grins. I'm pretty sure he's goading me to find out how serious I am about Amber.

"I'm not mating," I say firmly. "You both know I can't mate a human, even if she is a psychic." But my wolf disagrees. Lots of wolves mate humans; it must be possible. I'd just have to be careful not to give her a mating bite, or it could kill her. But mating a human would mean I'd lose my position as alpha. It would be seen as a sign of weakness. Our pups would have weak blood.

"Well, I'm ready to settle down." Trey yawns.

"You just want your dick sucked on the regular," Jared mutters.

"Yeah, so? Who doesn't?" Trey grabs the cushion he's sitting on and throws it at his pack brother.

"Guys," I warn them absently. My head spins with the idea of mating Amber. It's ridiculous, but now that it's on the table, my wolf won't stop salivating over the thought of having the prim little attorney as my own. I want to pull that bun down, tie her to my bed, and spread her legs. Spend so long eating her pussy she screams herself hoarse. Every night. For the rest of my life.

Not going to happen, buddy.

"Don't worry," Jared says. "We'll find another place to live after you bring the human to heel." He and Trey swap grins, and I want to punch both of them. They're having too much fun with this.

"In the meantime, we'll get earplugs or something," Trey adds.

"I already need earplugs." Jared throws a cushion at Trey. "You keep me up, howling while you jack off."

"I do not howl." Trey throws the cushion back and dives onto his pack mate, punching him through the cushion.

"Guys," I warn, and they stop. "Do me a favor. Sit tight on this. Amber's under my protection, but that doesn't mean she's my fucking mate."

"But she may become your fuck-mate." Jared grins like he knows I'm trying to figure out how to make it happen. "We'll let you warm her up to us first. When it's time, we'll make Trey wear a bag over his head."

The punching starts again. I grab my beer bottle before it goes flying, and watch them push at each other, hoping the crashing doesn't wake Amber up.

I know Trey and Jared are solid, but I don't want them

telling Tank, who will run to my dad. If my dad decides Amber is a threat, he won't hesitate to give a death order. For him, rules are rules. Life is black and white. I can just hear him lecturing me and Sedona, *That's how we survive.*

But no one is putting Amber down. I would fucking kill anyone who came near her. A growl rumbles in my chest at the thought.

But that doesn't mean I can have her, either.

4

Amber

I dream I'm being chased by a wolf. A huge, silver-eyed beast who morphs into a giant, ripped man. Who then catches me, pins me under his muscled body, and...

I wake up in the throes of orgasm.

Let the record reflect: *Full moons make werewolves get freaky.* Or am I the one who's getting freaky?

The bathroom mirror reflects my flushed cheeks. Apparently I love freaky.

Sighing, I drag a brush through my hair. Multiple visions, a horrible night out and then I meet a werewolf. Just another week in the life of Crazy Amber.

After two hours of frantically wiping down every surface in my apartment, I feel a bit better. Maybe I can just keep on keeping on, act normal. Garrett told me not to tell anyone, so I may as well pretend nothing happened. Right?

I mean, they're three huge, scary guys who happen to turn into wolves. Big deal. I turn into a monster once a month, too, when I'm on my period. Maybe I have more in common with Garrett than I thought.

Dressed for yoga, I grab my mat and head out the door, pausing to check if I packed my keys. My back and bottom tingle as if my body remembers Garrett pressing against me. He caught me when I almost fell, and walked me to my apartment, and taught me to a pick a lock. Keeping me safe. Taking care of me.

Do I pretend that never happened? What about the kiss and the spanking and his talented fingers between my legs?

I suck in a breath as my lady bits come to life with happy memories. Ducking my head to hide my blush, I practically run down the hall. No werewolves accost me on the way to my car. I'm almost disappointed.

Maybe I am back to Normal Amber's life. When I see Garrett, I'll just be cool.

Settling into my car, I'm about to back out of my spot when I see him. Massive shoulders stretching an army-green shirt, Garrett crosses his bulging arms over his chest. His head tilts to the side as he watches me.

I wave, ignoring the flip-flop of my heart. And then I hit the gas—only to have the car lurch forward. I forgot to put it in reverse. The front wheels of my Volvo hit the concrete block and roll over it, crunching the front of my car into the wall.

A second later, metal screams as my door rips off its hinges.

"Baby, are you okay?" Garrett leans over me, unclicking my seatbelt and pulling me from the car before folding me in his arms.

"Hey, neighbor." My voice comes out shaky. So much for being cool.

"What the hell?"

"You startled me. I, um—" Garrett's scent surrounds me, and calm settles my jangled nerves. My hands are splayed on his hard-muscled chest.

"Amber?"

Focus! Amber the Lawyer is never at a loss for words. "Are you, um, growling?"

"My wolf," Garrett says through a clenched jaw. "He's worried about you.'"

"Oh. Hi, wolf." I speak to Garrett's belly button. His shirt has ridden up, showing muscles the size of cobblestones.

More rumbles as Garrett laughs. The pleasant sound relaxes me. I'm standing in my hottie neighbor's arms, talking to his wolf. Nope, not crazy at all.

Garrett tucks an errant strand of hair behind my ear, brushes a thumb over the hill of my cheek, leans in, and kisses me.

At the touch of his lips, little shocks of lightning flash through me. I sigh and press forward, ready to rub myself against him. My hand slips under his shirt, caressing the smooth, sculpted muscle. Garrett angles his head, grips the back of my neck, and deepens the kiss. His tongue in my mouth stirs up parts of me down below.

The kiss goes on and on and when we finally break away, I can barely breathe. He holds me close with his firm hand on my neck and rests his forehead against mine.

I'm literally like the heroine of a Jane Austen romance, my chest heaving, about to swoon. "Um. Wow. Do all werewolves kiss like that?" I ask inanely. Really? Where is the sane Amber who always can verbally spar with the best of them in a courtroom?

Silver flashes through his eyes. "You won't be kissing any werewolves but me."

"Well no, of course not. I didn't mean to kiss you, either. You're the one who keeps doing it. I keep letting you."

"I'm glad you're okay." He releases the back of my neck, and I feel the loss. "I was worried there for a second."

"I see that." My door creaks as it hangs on one hinge. My front wheels are stuck between the concrete barrier and the wall. "What am I supposed to do now?"

"I'm surprised you don't have Triple A on speed dial, princess."

"I do, actually. But how do I explain those?" I point the deep imprints in the metal Garrett put there with his bare hands.

"I'll take care of it. Most of my pack are mechanics. They can get this straight."

"How are we going to get it back over the concrete barrier?"

Garrett's busy shooting off a text. By the time he's done, two big guys burst from the stairwell door. Again, I automatically step back.

"You remember Jared and Trey?"

"Hi, Counselor." Jared, the one with the shaved head and tattoo sleeves, nods.

The heavily pierced one actually grins at me before he points to my car. "This the problem?"

"Yep." Garrett pockets his cell phone. "Tank's coming with a tow truck. But I don't want to leave it until then."

The two punks walk to either side of my car.

"How's the weather?" Full Metal Face, also known as Trey, asks.

Garrett stands at the rear, sweeping a glance around the parking lot. "Old lady, three o'clock."

The three of them lean against my car, looking casual as

a woman crosses the parking lot, gets in her car, and drives off.

"All clear," Garrett murmurs.

The men all bend over and get a grip on my car before lifting it as if it weighs nothing. My jaw drops. Let the record reflect: *Werewolves have superhuman strength.* They carry it back into place, and set it gently down.

"Thanks, guys." Garrett nods, and the two punks wink at me and disappear before I find my voice.

"I guess that works."

"Tank will be here to tow it in a bit."

"Thank you," I say.

"You're welcome, princess."

So much for a normal Saturday. "I guess I'm going to miss yoga."

"I can help you with that."

"How? You going to teach me to hotwire a car?"

A grin, shake of his head. "I'll do you one better." He strides around a corner. The roar of motorcycle pipes herald his return.

"Oh no." I shake my head as he glides up on a huge black Harley. "No way I'm getting on that thing."

"Come on, Counselor." He tosses me a helmet. "Live a little."

~.~

Let the record reflect: *When riding a motorcycle, you should bring a change of panties.* Because they are basically vibrators. Really big vibrators.

I hold tight to Garrett, pressing into his back as the wind whips my hair below the helmet.

"Hey!" I shout as we motor away from downtown. "My yoga studio is in Armory Park!"

"Change of plans, princess," he tosses back, and pulls in at a little Mexican taco stand on the west side of the now dry Santa Cruz riverbed. "I'll take you to brunch."

I'd protest, but I'm not sorry. I would've been late for yoga, anyway, and even though I know it's a bad idea, I crave more time with my overbearing neighbor. Even if it is on a death machine. Which feels amazing between my thighs.

Garrett orders ten carne asada tacos, pays, and hands me the paper sack with our food. "Let's go."

"Where are we going?"

"For a picnic." He starts the motorcycle and takes the turn for A Mountain, leaning into a curve. The A is for the giant letter painted there—for University of Arizona—and I lean with him, trying to ignore the fact that I'm plastered against the hottest guy I've ever met. It's almost like I never had the morning orgasm at all.

We head up A Mountain, the statuesque saguaro cacti standing sentinel as we zoom past. The sun is high, but the air rushes past me, making the temperature perfect.

By the time Garrett pulls onto an overlook, I'm actually having fun. The view of the city and natural landscape beyond is incredible. Wrens chirp from their nests in the giant cacti. This is what it's like to be Garrett. Free.

The familiar knot of anxiety I always wear is gone, as if I've taken on his ease and strength. His overwhelming belief that the city belongs to him, and there's nothing he can't handle. I know I'm projecting, yet my gut tells me I'm right. What I feel is true. Garrett owns his life, downtown, this mountain.

But that's stupid. He may be a werewolf, but it doesn't make him invulnerable. "Shouldn't you be wearing a helmet?" I ask as I pull mine off.

"Worried about me, princess?"

"No," I mutter. "A wreck probably wouldn't make a dent in your hard head."

He just grins. "How did you like the ride?"

"It was nice." I flush.

"Glad I could pop your cherry. Your bike cherry."

I narrow my eyes and try not to think about what it would've been like if he'd been the guy who'd popped my actual cherry. So much better than Tommy Jackson.

He just laughs. "Come on, princess." He leads me to a picnic table. "Here. Dig in." He opens the container of tacos.

"Nice of you to ask me what I wanted," I mutter. "I could be on a diet. Or vegetarian."

He freezes, looking horrified. "Are you vegetarian?"

"No." My stomach growls.

"Thank the fates." He picks up a taco and devours it in one bite.

I'm suddenly worried there won't be enough for both of us. "But I am watching my weight."

He scoffs. "Why?"

"Same reason I go to yoga every week. It's what normal people do, you know, to keep in shape."

"I like your shape." His blue eyes sweep down from my face to my breasts and linger there. My nipples peak at the attention. "Tell you what, you eat—" he plunks a taco in front of me. "And I'll watch your weight."

"What?"

"I will watch it very, very closely." He ducks his head beneath the table to ogle my lower half.

I snap my knees shut, but a slow throb starts between

my legs. I imagine him under the table, prying my knees apart. Putting those sensual lips of his against my core. "I'm sure you will." Damn my voice for sounding breathy and excited. "Pass." I bite into the taco and moan. It is so good.

The man—werewolf—across the table looks like he wants to take a bite out of me.

Jesus, do werewolves bite? Why haven't I asked yet?

I nod to his fingers, the blue ink rendering of the moon in its various phases. "For someone who has a big secret, don't you think that tattoo is a little telling?"

He gives me a lopsided grin, one side of his mouth pulling up. "Most humans aren't like you, Amber."

It may not have been a compliment, but the way he looks at me makes my insides warm. "S-so, how does it work? Do you bite people to turn them during the full moon?"

Garrett gives a short bark of laughter. "We're not fucking leeches."

I stare blankly.

"Vampires."

My stomach knots. There are vampires, too? *Eeesh.*

"No, you're either born a shifter or you're not. You can't be *turned*. In fact, there are pathetically few of us left. Breeding with humans has caused our species to dwindle."

I suddenly long to know everything about them—meet the whole gang and understand what makes them tick. It hits me hard, like this is some knowledge I've been missing my whole life, that I should have known.

"I have a question for you, Counselor." Garrett has polished off six street tacos. "How do you drive if you get visions all the time?"

"I can suppress them. I don't usually get them unless I'm around big crowds of people. Or when I get touched."

He bares his teeth, like he can't stand the idea of anyone touching me. "How are you not a recluse, then?"

"I kind of am. I don't go out a lot, except to work and yoga. Foxfire is my only close friend." My life sounds pathetic. Normal Amber is pretty lame.

"Why did you choose to become a lawyer?"

I square my shoulders. "Why? Because I could've been a fortune-teller instead?"

He laughs. "No, baby. Somehow, I can't see you doing that. I'm just wondering what makes a hot, talented woman like you go into such a rigid occupation."

He means I'm too uptight. I touch my tangled waves, wanting the security of my usual French twist. "I work with kids in the system, getting them out of bad situations."

"Isn't that *pro bono* stuff?"

"Almost," I admit. "I'm lucky I got scholarships for law school, otherwise I couldn't afford my student loans and rent."

"I didn't know you were such a humanitarian type."

"Yep. Foxfire calls me a bleeding heart liberal. But I want to give back, and if I can help these kids navigate the system, save them from what I—" I stop short. I didn't mean to tell him about that.

"Save them..." Garrett prompts when I don't go on. "What were you going to say?"

I set down the rest of my second street taco. Should I tell him? "I was in the system." I swallow a lump in my throat. "Foster care, from the time I was six."

His fingers wrap into fists, jaw sets tight. He looks one part sick, one part furious. "Are you fucking kidding me?"

"Easy, Hulk."

He exhales a measured breath and stands up.

I watch him walk around the table and plunk down on the concrete bench beside me, straddling it.

He reaches for me, using one giant paw to swivel my knees in his direction, turning me in my seat. Leaving his hand on my knee, he cups my nape with the other. His brow knits with concern. "You okay?" His voice is gruff, like he's going to go back in time and kick the ass of anyone who hurt me in my past.

"Yeah." I let out a shaky breath. I can't believe I told him. It violates my number one rule for keeping Crazy Amber under wraps. It took Foxfire years of prying to get it out of me. "Foster care saved me, but it wasn't easy. I tried my best to act normal, but I kept getting sent back because they thought I was crazy. You know, because of the..."

"The visions?"

"Yeah. My last set of foster parents thought I had a drug problem." I shake my head. "They spent years trying to medicate me."

"Did it help?"

"No. It made me feel worse. But they meant well. And my life in foster care was so much better than the alternative."

"So, now you work with kids, making sure they get the life they deserve." His eyes are the deepest blue, filled with understanding. I don't want to accept it, but it feels so damn good.

"Yes." I'm grateful he changed the subject back to work. Work is safe. I launch into a long explanation of my state job as child's attorney, representing kids in the foster system.

"Sounds intense," he says. "It also sounds like you're really making a difference. Not bad for a slimy lawyer." He tries for light, but his eyes still hold a world of grief on my behalf.

I roll my eyes and give his sturdy chest a light shove.

He catches my wrists and pins them together with a large hand. "None of that, bad girl."

Oh, lordy. The memory of my spanking last night comes rushing back. As if it hadn't been at the forefront of my mind all day.

"No disrespect." His voice drops an octave. "Or I'll have to punish you again."

My pussy clenches, but I ignore the way the threat lights me up.

He drops his gaze to my pebbled nipples showing through my tight yoga tank, ratting me out.

My face heats. "Y-you're the bad one. Not me." I yank the container of tacos closer. "There are two left, Aren't you going to eat them?" It's a lame attempt at distraction, but he allows it.

"So, if you were having lunch with a business owner who wants to give back to the community, what would you say foster kids need most?"

I straighten. "Does this business owner happen to own property all over Tucson? Including Club Eclipse?"

He grins. "Maybe."

"Believe it or not, I'd love to have access to the club one night."

He quirks a sexy brow. "Really?"

"Really. One of the social workers for the foster kids is looking for a place to host a "Families' Night Out" with kids and their foster parents. It'd be so cool to take them to Eclipse. Let them have a dance party."

"I don't serve alcohol to anyone under twenty one," he deadpans.

"Of course not," I swat his hand. In a blur of movement,

he catches it. My lips part as his mouth closes over my fingers, sucking them. The slow roll of his tongue has me blushing. Once more I imagine that tongue working between my legs. Not that I've ever wanted that before. Hell, I'd always thought it was kind of disgusting. You know, unsanitary. But the velvet wet heat of Garrett's mouth has me dying for it.

I sag in my seat when he lets me go.

Swallowing hard, I continue. "I-it'd be a dry event. Just sodas and music. Maybe a light show. The kids would think it's so cool. It'll be good neutral territory for them to bond with their new families."

"All right," he says slowly. "I'll see what I can do."

"Would your roommates volunteer to help?"

"Jared and Trey?" His eyebrows pop up. "They'll do whatever I tell them to do."

"You said it yourself: they're Boy Scouts. They'd be great role models. As long as they tell the kids not to drink or smoke, and to stay in school."

"My buddy Tank owns a motorcycle shop. He has a handful of high school kids who hang out on the regular to learn from him. I've always thought it could be a formal program. You know—vocational training or something."

My heart squeezes to hear that Garrett—the giant werewolf I'd so misjudged—thinks about helping local teens. "That's an incredible idea. Would you want to be a part of it?"

He shrugs. "Yeah."

I picture him mentoring young would-be thugs and giving them a sense of purpose and confidence. "I bet you'll make a great dad," I blurt. My eyes widen when I realize I just brought up having kids on our first date. I don't even know what made me say it. Yes, I do. My overactive ovaries, which are still dropping eggs every two minutes in hopes they'll get lucky with him. "I mean—"

"Yeah, I'll teach them to pick locks and ride motorcycles. Isn't that what every woman looks for in the father of her pup?" There's a challenge in his voice, and a flush of shame runs through me for being so judgmental of him.

"I'm sorry I acted like a snooty bitch when we met. I was just nervous about my safety and I—"

He cuts me off with a kiss, stamping his lips over mine with an unspoken demand.

I yield, opening for his tongue, trying to ignore the way the Earth tilts on its axis and dumps me on my butt. Somehow, I know my hair is never going to fit back into the uptight twist I used to wear.

"Oh, Amber," Garrett breaks the kiss. "If you had any idea all the terrible things I want to do to you, you'd know you were right to be nervous."

My breasts ache now, nipples stinging and chafing against the fabric of my yoga top. I want his mouth on them. I want to know all the terrible things. He's already spanked me. What else is the kinky werewolf into? Bondage? Humiliation? I never considered anything but plain old missionary sex to be in my future, but it's like a door has slid open, showing me a whole new, beautiful world.

I grope for something to say, something safe and neutral. "What about you?" I bump his foot with mine. "How did you get into real estate?"

"I moved to Tucson when I was eighteen. My dad gave me a startup loan, and I bought a small commercial property and rented it out. Did all the repairs and fixup myself. Then I got lucky. Downtown revitalization took off, and the value of the property shot through the roof. I borrowed against equity to pay my dad back and open Eclipse. My dad was disappointed to say the least."

"That you opened a nightclub?"

"Yeah. He says I'll always be a punk."

A rush of anger runs through me on Garrett's behalf. I may have jumped to the same conclusion when I met Garrett, but I've since seen he's more than a motorcycle-driving hoodlum. And even with a startup loan from his father, any guy who could grow his real estate empire from one commercial building to a multi-million dollar empire has some business skills and savvy.

Garrett's smile doesn't reach his eyes. "Guess he's right."

Hearing about his father's condemnation suddenly gives me some insight into why Garrett hasn't grown up. With a father like that, you'd either want to prove him wrong or prove him right. Looks like Garrett chose proving him right. Yes, he's a little old to be rebelling, but if he grew up with an overbearing, judgmental asshole for a parent, I can see how that might stick with him.

"So, what's the average day look like for you?"

"Drink beer. Harass my hot neighbor." He keeps playing the thug role.

I yank the container of tacos away just as he reaches for one. He arches a stern brow. I stifle a grin and shove them back, eyeing his enormous pecs.

He catches me looking and smirks. "Like what you see, angel?"

I shrug like his nearness has no effect on me. "You work out for those?"

"Naw. This is all genetics, baby." He flexes, showing off his giant biceps. I wonder how many girls at Eclipse throw themselves at his feet every night. The thought makes me want to strangle all of them.

"Run the club? Manage your properties?" I continue pressing.

"Nope, I have pack members and employees to do that, now. I manage them."

Pack members. He has a pack of shifters. I don't know why, but I love that idea. The men who seemed so intimidating and rough in the elevator that first day, the tough bouncers at the club, they're not motorcycle club members. Or maybe they are, but they're also pack members. Wolf pack members.

I suddenly wonder if every motorcycle club is actually made up of werewolves. I'm too embarrassed of my ignorance to ask.

I wonder if they dress like punks on purpose. To warn humans off or something. Not that I'm complaining, today. His massive body is drool worthy in his signature ripped jeans and faded T-shirt that reads *Dark Side of the Moon*.

Moon. Heh. I wonder how much moon paraphernalia he collects.

"Eat your taco, Counselor." Garrett has polished off the remaining two and points at my second, half-eaten one.

"I'm full."

"Then come with me." He tugs me up, his huge hand swallowing mine. Strong fingers, powerful enough to crush metal, but so gentle with me.

He leads me up the mountain, away from the motorcycle. We're off the beaten path, and when it proves too tricky for my tennis shoes, he lifts and carries me easily over the rocky terrain, to the very top of A Mountain then sets me down on a small boulder. The view is even more spectacular.

"Is this what you wanted to show me?" I ask.

"I just wanted to change things up." He fingers a lock of

my hair. "What you told me on the picnic table—about being in foster care—do you tell many people that?"

I swallow. "No."

"Are you close with your foster parents?"

"The last ones? The ones who tried to medicate me? Not really. I think I went to law school just to prove I didn't need their help or anyone else's."

"Do you have any close friends? Anyone who knows you're psychic?"

"Just Foxfire. At least, she's the only one who believes me when I tell her what I've seen."

"Anyone else?"

I shake my head. My chest hurts a little. "Why are you asking me these questions?"

"Now I know why you're wound so tight, baby. Your gift makes you isolate from others. You have no one to watch your back."

"It's not a gift." My throat clogs.

"And you don't have anyone to share your secret with. No family. No pack," he murmurs as if talking to himself.

The pain under my breastbone expands until I blink back tears.

He catches my expression. "Fuck. I didn't mean to upset you." He pulls me to stand and wraps me in his arms.

I resist, hating weakness.

He ignores my attempts to push him away, his strength making me seem like a toddler. "I just want to know what makes you tick. I don't want to hurt you, Amber."

"You can't hurt me," I declare, but it's an old assertion. The cousin to *I don't need anyone*, and I know it's not true. I give up resistance and sag against him, resting my cheek on his massive chest. I wipe my eyes.

"I won't let anyone hurt you again."

I want to call *bullshit* on that. But I like the way it sounds. And I like the way it feels to lean into his warm strength and soak it up.

I've never opened up to anyone the way I did to Garrett. I'm not even sure how he got me to. But I trust him. More than I've ever trusted anyone in my life. "Well." My voice sounds shaky. "I guess we both know each other's secrets now."

"Yep." He sets his chin on the top of my head. We fit perfectly. "Your secret's safe with me, princess."

For a moment, we stay like that, molded together, looking down on Tucson. Garrett inhales through his nose, and his hands tighten on me. One wanders down to my ass, squeezing my buns through my skin-tight yoga pants.

"You had to be wearing *these*." Both hands grip my ass now, squeezing and releasing, circling and caressing. I remember the way he stroked my ass after he lit it on fire last night, and a dark hunger burns in my lower belly.

He lifts me to straddle his waist. His mouth falls on my shoulder, half bite, half kiss. He lifts and lowers my ass, rubbing my core over the massive bulge of his cock. "I can feel your hot little pussy, baby. Are you even wearing panties?"

"No," I manage to say through panting breaths. I've never wanted a man so badly in my life. I've never surrendered like this—just let a guy lead and do whatever he wants.

A rumble sounds in Garrett's chest.

I draw back and see his eyes are silver. "Your wolf is showing," I murmur.

"Fuck." He drops me to the ground and stares at me, fingers balling into fists at his sides.

"What's wrong? You okay?"

He doesn't answer. A muscle in his jaw jumps. He mutters a curse and pulls off his shirt.

Dayum. His arms—the muscles are almost as big as my head. The sight of his eight pack makes me want to howl at the moon. He has a wolf paw tattoo on his shoulder.

"What are you doing?" I cross my arms in front of me to hide my tight nipples. His fingers go to his belt next. I throw out my hand. "Hold up, big guy. What are you doing?" Does he think we're having sex, right here, right now?

"I need to shift."

"Here? Now?" I glance around. "Garrett, no." The sound of a car below reaches us. "It's broad daylight, and anyone could come up."

He steps close, his scent washing over me. "I can't help it. You bring the change on. If I don't let the wolf out, I'm going to put you on your hands and knees and"—he cuts himself off with a dog-like a shake of his head—"do those terrible things."

Please—do them.

His skin ripples in terrifying motion.

"No." I put my palms on his chest, as if I can stop the wolf from coming out. "Stop, please." I know what it's like to be a kid, and to see things I'm not supposed to see. "Don't do this. Not like this."

"Can't stop." His voice comes out choked. He's going to shift in front of me, right now.

"Stay with me, Garrett," I do the only thing I can think of. Surging up to tiptoe, I wrap my arms around his neck and kiss him.

Heat blasts through me as soon as our lips touch. He lifts me, fists a hand in my hair, and tugs my head back. The swell of his hardened cock presses against my belly. The kiss ignites my body, sensation blasting through me. Everything in me comes alive.

"The things I want to do to you." The raw hunger in his expression is unnerving.

"You can," I promise, and I mean it. I want it. "Just not here. Take me home. You don't have to shift." I don't know if it's my intuition or fear speaking, but there's an urgency to keeping him sane, preventing whatever he's wrestling with from happening.

He licks up my throat, my head still immobilized in his iron grasp. His lips drag across my jaw; he nips my mouth. My body responds, hips pushing up against him, the heat of my core seeking something to grind on.

He bites my shoulder so hard, I cry out in pain. It seems to jerk him out of his lust-filled stupor, and he releases me, jumping back as if I'd burned him.

"Fuck, Amber." His eyes are still silver. He drags a hand through his blond hair, breathing hard. "Fuck. Did I hurt you? Fuck!"

"No. No, you didn't." It's a partial truth. I lean forward, missing him already. My hands want to stay molded to that incredible chest. "It's okay—" I reach for him. I know what it's like to feel out of control.

"No." Fury mars his handsome face. "It can't happen again. This was a bad idea." He's breathing heavily. "I need to stay away."

"Garrett—"

"I can't be near you." He passes a hand over his face. His shoulders hunch. A large pop sounds. "Too close to a full moon. I've got to go." He whirls, striding down the other side of the mountain. Away from the road. Away from me.

"Wait!" Is he just going to leave me here? I can't drive a

freakin' motorcycle. I scramble after him. "What happens during the full moon?"

His growl echoes off the boulders as he disappears, stopping me in my tracks. "I go hunting."

~.~

LET THE RECORD REFLECT: *The werewolf abandoned his date on A Mountain.*

"Thanks for picking me up," I tell Foxfire as she pulls away from the overlook. The site of a date gone awry. I'd waited a full hour for Garrett to return before accepting I'd have to find my own ride back.

"No problem. Least I could do, after making a fool of myself last night." She looks a bit wan but steadier than I feel. "Tell me again what happened. You went on a date and, in the middle of it, he up and left?"

"He's...strange." *Understatement of the year.* And hot. And probably a millionaire. And a werewolf.

And a goddamn asshole.

"Wait," Foxfire says. "I'm putting together the pieces. Is this your neighbor?"

"Yeah."

"And he was there last night, right?"

"He owns Club Eclipse. And, after I got home, we had a little talk." And a little spanking, followed by a not-so-little orgasm. And hot dreams all night long.

I press my hands to my cheeks to hide my blush.

"He kinda knocked on my door. I got scared and went

out the fire escape. I nearly fell, and he caught me. Brought me to his apartment and told me—" I break off.

"To never set foot in his club again," Foxfire fills in my awkward pause. "Because of me."

"No, it's fine. I think he'd let us back in." He told me we could use the club for the foster fun night. I hope he meant it. "This morning, he helped me with my car, but then..."

"He took you for a ride on his motorcycle and stranded you in the middle of nowhere."

"Yes," I rub my head. My temples throb like another vision is due. Wonderful.

"This guy sounds like bad news. You're usually not the reckless one."

"I know." What was I thinking? "We have this connection."

"What could you possibly have in common with this guy? He's in a motorcycle gang. You spend nights working or organizing your pens and ironing your underwear."

"Gee thanks. Why don't you just call me boring?"

"You know what I mean, Amber. I love you to bits, but you're a control freak. That guy is chaos."

"You don't get it. I felt like I could open up to him. I told him about the visions."

"Really?" Foxfire's eyebrows arch so high they almost disappear under her bangs.

"Yeah. He's the first person I've told in years, other than you." Foxfire's grandmother was a medicine woman, so she grew up hearing about the spiritual side of things. It's one of the reason we're so close.

"I can't believe you confided in that jerkoff. He seems likes the big Neanderthal type."

"He is, but he's more than that. I had an episode in front of him, and he took care of me."

"When you told him about the visions, how did he react?"

My head swims at the word *vision* and I put a hand on the dash to steady myself. "He believed me."

"What'd you see?" Foxfire asks.

"A wolf." Something flashes in the desert as I stare out the window. A coyote or some other wild animal? Garrett is out there, running in his other form. For a moment, I taste the hot, dry air, powering past cacti as I run on all fours. I'm a predator, powerful, unafraid. The moon hovers just under the horizon, unseen, but my skin tingles as it calls to me, telling me to shift...

"Did you just say werewolf?" Foxfire's gasp brings me back into the car.

"No." I shake my head, dazed. Did I just have a vision? "Um, what'd I just say?"

"You said *Garrett is a werewolf.* At least I think that's what you said. You were kinda out of it."

Damn. "Uh...that's the name of his motorcycle club, I think. The Werewolves. They have a wolf theme. Club Eclipse. Moon tattoos. It's a thing." *Please, please, believe me.*

"Okay, whatever."

I stay quiet, just focusing on breathing. Foxfire weaves into traffic as the desert slowly makes way for urban sprawl. I close my eyes, fighting dizziness.

"Does your head hurt?" Foxfire asks.

"A little."

"You look a little sick, otherwise I'd take you apartment hunting, right now."

I slide down in my seat. Do I want to leave my apartment? Not have Garrett as a neighbor? No. He fucked up today, but so did I. Was there ever more proof I'm a freak?

"I don't like this, Amber." Foxfire's frown creates furrows alongside her mouth. "Garrett sounds like bad news."

"It's okay," I tell her. "I think he'll stay away from me from now on." I ignore the pang in my heart. I barely know the guy. I shouldn't care if I never see him again.

"Just take me home." My voice breaks on the word. I can't lie to myself. Years of foster care, and I've never had a safe place to call home. A place I can be myself, a family who accepts me for what I am.

That's why spending time with Garrett was so special. For a few short hours, I felt like I belonged.

5

Garrett

I made it home, no thanks to you. Just thought you should know.

I read Amber's text as I enter my apartment building. For a second, I debate texting a reply, but I fire one off to my sister instead.

It's been almost a day since you checked in. Call me soon.

I pocket my phone before I crush it in my grip. *Females.* Maybe it's a good thing my pack is all male.

My wolf surges forward as I pass the spot where Amber's car was parked. I push him back down. Hours of running, chasing jackrabbits, and I'm still all riled up. One woman is the cause of this. I catch her sweet scent in the stairwell, and I'm ready to rampage.

Mate.

There's no other reason I should act like this. I've never had problems with my wolf before. But, one date with Amber, and I almost lost control. I was ready to rip her clothing from her, throw her down and fuck her senseless.

Worse, my canines had elongated, ready to mark her forever with my scent. Claim her as mine so no other wolf would ever think about taking her. The trouble is—she's human. Mating her would mean relinquishing my position as alpha. An alpha mates an alpha. Humans are about as far from alpha as it gets. Although a psychic human might be different. If we produced dominant wolf pups with psychic abilities, it would be epic. But the pack isn't going to wait around to see what our pups look like. If they sense a leader has a weakness, another dominant wolf moves in. Tank. Or Jackson King, the lone wolf who owns the multi-billion dollar tech company SeCure.

No, I need to resist Amber. For her good, and mine. Hell, I could've hurt her. I had zero control, was ready to tear her flesh with my teeth to make sure she knew who claimed her.

There's a word for wolves who lose it like this: moon mad. The wolf takes over, consumed with the desire to mate. The more dominant the wolf, the more dangerous it is.

I'm alpha. I'm the most dominant wolf I know, except maybe my dad. It's clear my wolf wants Amber. To keep from going mad, I'll have to either claim her or stay way far away.

I take the stairs. I was out all night, running, trying to tire my wolf out before I had to get close to Amber again. No such luck. My animal goes crazy as I open the door to the hall. Not to mention my libido. My erection presses painfully against my jeans.

Amber's door opens. Her name leaps to my lips, but out comes a tiny woman with rainbow-colored hair. She shuts the door carefully with one hand, the other steadying a large, floppy purse as she starts down the hall. At the last minute, she looks up when I pass her.

"You!" She stops to put her hands on her hips to glare up at me. "What's your deal?"

"Excuse me?" My wolf would normally snarl at the challenge to my authority, but this little lady smells like Amber. "Who are you?" I say, just as I recognize her from the club the night before.

"Foxfire. I'm Amber's friend. I picked her up in the mountains where you stranded her." Her finger almost pokes me in the chest.

My throat vibrates with a growl. "Sweetheart, you need to back off."

"You need to stay away from my girl. You and your werewolf gang—"

"What?" I almost roar.

She throws up her hands. "Whatever the name of your gang is. Wolves or Werewolves or whatever. You can call yourself the Dumbass Jackholes for all I care. Just leave Amber alone." With the final shout, she stomps off, leaving me trembling, my skin crackling with the desire to shift and tear apart the threat to my pack.

Amber let my secret slip. I trusted her, and the first thing she does is tell her spitfire friend, who then shouts it to the world.

"Oh, hell, no." I march to Amber's door, clenching my fist tight. She wants to see the big bad wolf? "Amber? Open up."

If she goes out the fire escape again, she'll be sorry.

The scent of vanilla and sweet orange.

"Open the door, Amber,"

"What are you going to do?" I hear the patter of her heartbeat even through the wood.

"Open it now. One... two..."

The lock clicks open. Her face is pinched and pale.

"Wise decision." I push past her into her living room.

She trails behind me.

I stop, clenching my fists as if it will help me keep my wolf in line. I don't know what the hell to do. I don't want to threaten her with the old-school consequence of a human knowing our secret—death. I'd take a bullet through the head before I let anyone harm this beautiful human.

"You broke your word to me."

She stands, shoulders hunched, eyes on the floor.

The submissive pose flips a switch in me. My cock turns hard as stone, despite my disappointment. Genuine anger changes to a lusty desire to paint her ass red. Right before I bend her over and pound her from behind.

"I didn't mean to tell her," she whispers. "I slipped into a vision and...it just came out. I told her it was the name of your motorcycle gang."

Some of the tension in my face eases. I review what Foxfire said, and it fits. Still, I don't want anyone thinking we're wolves, whether it's the name of a gang or the real animal. "Well, we don't have a gang. What are you going to tell her when she finds out we don't call ourselves that, even in jest?"

She shrinks down even more. Normally, she wouldn't be this cowed, but I sense the shame in her scent. She's truly sorry.

My chest rumbles with my wolf as I prowl around her. "I don't think you understand. Shifters do not allow humans to know they exist. It is common practice to *eliminate* any threats to our privacy."

Amber still hasn't moved. I'm not sure she's breathing at all. My wolf loves dominating her, even though the human part of me scrambles to keep control. Images of pinning her delicate hands to the wall and smacking that cute ass flood my brain.

"You were already in danger, Amber. I liked you, so I was willing to go out on a limb and let you live. But now there are two of you who know. You just put your friend into grave danger."

"Please don't hurt Foxfire." A tear streaks down her cheek. The salty scent of it subdues my irritation faster than a tranquilizer dart. Another sign she's my mate.

I run my fingers through her hair, gripping a handful and slowly drawing her head back, exposing her neck. For a second, my vision goes dark, as I fight the animal growling at me to *mark her.*

"Naughty, Amber," I breathe in her ear, catching a note of arousal to her frightened scent.

It spikes my own. I let her feel the weight of my dominance. Let her understand how dangerous a creature I really am. "What am I going to do with you?"

My phone rings, breaking the spell. I step back and yank it from my pocket. I see Sedona's name on the screen and answer it quickly.

"Why in the hell haven't I heard from you until now?"

"Uh," a male voice says. "This is Jason, Sedona's friend. We're in San Carlos?"

Ice shoots through my veins. "Yeah?"

"Sedona...well, she kind of disappeared."

"What do you mean, *kind of disappeared?* Where is she?"

"We don't know. She went out for a run on the beach, and she never came back. We've looked everywhere. We even tried the cops, but they didn't seem like they cared that much. We were thinking maybe you could call the embassy or something?"

Sedona. My sister. Gone.

My animal rises in me, clawing to the surface. Amber's worried face appears in front of me. I focus on her.

"I'm coming," I growl, my voice half gone to my wolf. "Where?"

The kid gets what I'm asking and promises to text the directions. The thought that I have to wait to know where to go is the only thing that keeps me from crushing my phone.

"What is it?" Amber's voice shakes. And she should be scared. She woke a big bad predator, and now she's going to have to deal with the consequences. I stalk forward, and she backs up, like the good prey that she is.

"My sister, Sedona. She's missing."

"Oh no." Her eyes go wide. Her back hits the wall, but she never stops meeting my gaze. "What happened?"

In answer, I press my forearms on either side of her head, caging her in. My body covers hers. One move and my cock will brush against her, and I'll lose it. My hands fist, fighting for control. I drop my head, inhaling her warm, sweet scent. *Amber. Mate.* She's the only thing holding me together right now.

She's the only one with the power to tear me apart.

"Garrett?" My name on her lips makes me want to forget my failings as a brother and my terror over Sedona's disappearance. I want to breathe in Amber, and her alone.

Instead, I back up enough she can see the light silver in my eye. "Pack a bag and grab your passport. We're going to Mexico."

"What?"

"You're psychic. You see thing others don't. You're coming with me to find her."

"I'm sorry, Garrett, but I can't. I have work on Monday—"

"I'm not asking. You broke the rules, little human. I can't

let you run around free, and I have to go, which means you're coming along. I own you now."

~.~

Amber

I huddle in the backseat of Garrett's Range Rover, shivering, even though it's not cold. The doors on either side of me open, and Jared and Trey slide in, sandwiching me between them.

Let the record reflect: *I'm not into foursomes or kidnap scenarios.* I guess I should have told Garrett that, because this is not my idea of a great second date.

"What's with the lawyer, boss? She doesn't look happy to be here."

"She's coming with us. Don't let her escape," Garrett growls. He climbs into the front seat and peels out of the parking lot. I scramble to click in my seat belt. My two bodyguards—because that's what they are—don't bother.

The tattooed one—Jared—sits and watches me, arms braced as Garrett weaves in and out of traffic. "What's your plan with her?"

"I'm sitting right here," I mutter.

"We gonna have to kill her?" Trey rumbles.

They're joking. I'm pretty sure. But not positive. *Fuck.*

"If he wanted to kill her, she'd already be dead, and we'd be disposing of the body," Jared says, as I choke on my own breath.

"No killing. She's gonna help us." Garrett's deep rumble stirs me even in this tense moment.

"Oh yeah." Jared studies me. He has long eyelashes and hazel eyes. "I forgot—she's psychic."

"You told them?"

Garrett's eyes meet mine in the rear view mirror. "I don't hide anything from my pack."

Oh, so no reciprocity here? I bite back a retort. Now is not the time for Lawyer Amber to assert her case. Maybe when the energy in the car isn't thick with tension. I can barely breathe.

"You think you can sense a missing person, psychic lady?" Jared asks. One of his tattoos is a skeleton amorously entangled with a very buxom, half-naked lady. *Charming.*

"My name is Amber. " I pull out my snooty voice to bolster myself against fear. "And the answer is no. It's not a skill I know how to use. It's more like something that happens to me."

"Well, I need you to try," Garrett says from the front seat.

"I really don't know how." I don't. And I know he's going to blame me when it doesn't work.

"So, why is she our prisoner?" Trey pushes.

I stiffen at the casual way he asks, as if taking prisoners is par for the course.

"She talked," Garrett mutters.

"You're scaring her." Jared puts an arm around me and lightly rubs my shoulder. "She's shaking like a leaf."

"Do *not* touch her." Garrett's growl makes my stomach drop to my feet. His eyes glow silver in the mirror.

Jared removes his arm.

Trey shifts in his seat, putting a few inches between me and his big body. "Yes, sir."

"Understood, boss," Jared echoes.

They look like punks, but they sound like they're in the military.

Garrett's not done. "If either of you touches her I will smash your faces in, got it?"

Neanderthal. These guys are total Neanderthals. But my entire body flushes, and some part of me enjoys his possessive threat. Or is it just protective? Either way, it puts a warm, squirmy feeling in my belly.

"So, if she tries to escape, I'll just stop her with my invisible forcefield," Trey mutters.

"Are you really talking back to me?" Garrett demands. His fingers are white on the steering wheel.

"No, sir." Trey exchanges a glance with Jared, raising his eyebrows slightly, as if to say, "What's with him?"

I breathe a little easier after seeing this exchange.

"Amber has a friend." I tense all over again at Garrett's words. "Her name is Foxfire. She was at the club."

"Miss Pukes-alot? I remember," Jared says.

"Call Tank and tell him to keep an eye on her."

"What?" I blurt before I think. "No."

"Yes—"

"Foxfire's harmless. She thinks Werewolves is the name of your motorcycle gang or something. I swear, she won't tell anyone." My voice rises to match my level of desperation.

"You told someone about us?" Trey asks. The way the temperature drops in the car, I realize how serious this is. I'm in big trouble.

"I had a vision. It slipped out. Don't take it out on Foxfire."

"No harm will come to your friend," Garrett promises. "I swear on my wolf."

"I just need her address." Jared pauses mid text.

I shake my head. Tears burn my eyes. Stupid, stupid visions. Stupid werewolves. I didn't ask for any of this. "Please," I whisper.

"Amber."

I meet Garrett's eyes in the mirror.

He says nothing more, but his look demands I yield into his inflexible will. Maybe I have Stockholm syndrome. With a sigh, I tell them Foxfire's address.

"She'll be okay," Garrett assures me.

"Yeah, don't worry," Trey adds.

We drive in silence for forty minutes, until we pass the sign for the Mexican border. A jolt runs through me when I see it. Am I really going to leave the country with these wolves?

"Amber, look at me." Garrett taps the rearview mirror until I meet his eyes. "No trouble," he warns. "Do not call attention to us in any way. Don't speak unless you're asked a direct question. Do not give them any cause to stop us, understand?"

I tighten my lips. My heart races. I'm in serious trouble. Kidnapped by a lethal pack of wolves and taken to Mexico. Am I ever coming back? Lawyer Amber would never allow herself to be taken out of the country by near strangers. She got a top score on the bar exam. She's not stupid. At what point did I check in my brain and start thinking with my vagina? I don't let anyone push me around, hot werewolf, or not.

"Are we clear?"

I force myself to nod, before looking away. I need to think of something, quick. This is nuts, and I've spent a life-time trying to keep Crazy Amber out of my life.

Our car inches forward in line. When we reach the little concrete hut, Garrett turns off the car, signaling that we all need to get out to bring our paperwork inside. He claps a large hand on my shoulder as we walk forward.

Inside, he continues to direct me. I fill out the tourist

visa form, and bring it forward when the man behind the counter motions to me.

"*Disculpe.*" I pray Garrett doesn't speak Spanish. His grip tightens as I rush on. "*Tengo un problema...*"

A rumble comes from Garrett, low but distinct. A warning.

I gulp down my words. What the hell am I doing, anyway?

"*Em...dónde está el baño?*" I ask for the bathroom instead of explaining my problem. and Garrett eases his grip.

The man points toward the *Damas* sign on the restroom.

I bob my head. "*Gracias.*"

When the man hands the paperwork back, I head to the restroom, Garrett on my heels.

"I'll be right out," I tell him.

Inside, I explore my options. Like many buildings in Mexico, the little concrete structure is simply made, with screen-less windows near the ceiling that hinge open. It'll be tight, but I might be able to fit through the small opening. I stand on the toilet and hoist myself up, throwing my leg toward the window. I fall short and drop back to the ground, panting.

Come on, Amber. You can do this.

Another try, and I manage to hook my ankle over the edge of the open window. My heart races like a humming-bird's as I inch my leg through to the knee then hang onto the top of the stall and swing my other leg up. Slowly, I push my body forward, on an angle to fit through the narrow passage. I have no idea what's outside. Probably a border guard with a machine gun who will assume I'm a criminal. But I speak Spanish. I can present my case. No, better to not incriminate the werewolves. I'll just tell them I don't feel well and need to get a cab back to Tucson or something like that. Someone here will gladly take my money.

I wriggle and turn, propelling myself through the window. Sucking in a breath, I lay my middle across the narrow ledge of the window.

A hand closes around my ankle, and I scream, jerking and smacking my head on the ceiling. I twist to see who grabbed me, but my own body blocks my view. I try to kick free, and for a moment, I almost succeed, but then two hands grip my hips, lifting me from the perch and pulling me out.

Garrett. Only a shifter is this strong.

I slide down his hard, muscled body. Landing on the ground, I face two hundred pounds of disgruntled male. "What did I tell you about running from a wolf?"

My nipples are hard from dragging down his chest. His clean scent lures me in, reminding me of the night he carried me up to his apartment and spanked my ass pink. I must be nuts, because half of me hopes he'll punish me that way again. I draw in a shaky breath. "It was worth a try."

He quirks a brow, slipping his arms around me and pulling me close to his hard frame.

I stifle a moan.

"Listen, I know I'm an asshole to drag you down here. I know you're freaking out. But you can't run away from me. My wolf will chase, and that could be dangerous for you. Besides, I need your help." He stabs his fingers through his hair, leaving it rumpled.

His emotions are palpable to me. I never considered myself empathic in addition to clairvoyant, but with him, it seems I am. "I-I don't even know where we're going."

He brushes a lock of hair back from my eyes. "We're

going to San Carlos, where my sister disappeared this morning. She's a werewolf, too, and she vanished into thin air."

"But... who can kidnap a werewolf?"

His jaw tenses, but he draws in a slow breath and exhales. "I don't know. But we need to find her. Soon."

The image of a terrified wolf lying on her side, surrounded by men flashes before my eyes. Ice floods my veins.

Garrett is telling the truth.

~.~

Garrett

I toss Jared the keys. "You drive." I lead Amber to the backseat and climb in beside her.

I pull out my phone and open the photos on it, scrolling through until I find one of my sister and show it to Amber. "This is Sedona. She went out for a run on the beach and didn't come back."

Amber looks at the picture and nibbles her lip. "You think I'll be able to figure out where she is?"

"Will you just see if you get anything? Anything at all?"

She stares at the phone but doesn't seem to be looking at the picture. Her eyes are unfocused.

I force down a stab of frustration and wait.

Finally, she says in a shaky voice, "What if I see something you don't want to know?"

"What do you see?"

She looks past me out the window, a haunted expression in her eyes.

"What?"

"I saw a white wolf, on her side, suffering. Surrounded by men."

My wolf nearly breaks out of me. My whole body shakes with the almost change. My growl vibrates through the car.

I blink, but when I look over, Amber's almost in Trey's lap.

"Stay quiet, eyes down," he whispers to her.

Why the fuck is she in his arms?

I reach out and haul her into my lap. "I said *don't touch her*." My voice is choked with wolf.

"You scared her, boss." Trey keeps his own eyes lowered, his voice quiet and even. "Don't fight him," he warns Amber, and I realize the little human is struggling in my arms.

I ease my grip. "Sorry." One last inhale of her signature Amber scent, and I let her slide off my lap to her seat.

She starts to raise her gaze but drops her eyes again, holding still like a rabbit who thinks she can't be seen by the hawk above.

I unclench my fists and reach out to stroke her hair.

She doesn't move. "I told you. No one wants to know the things I see."

"No, I do." I'm about to apologize again, when I catch the scent of her tears. My wolf whines and backs down. It's almost a relief not to feel the power of the animal clamoring for freedom. As my brain and logic return, I'm flooded with sympathy for this sweet human who obviously considers her gift a curse. How she's suffered for this skill. The need to protect and care for her outweighs the danger facing Sedona, which I can do nothing about at the moment. I cup her chin with a gentle touch and lift her face. "You've seen a lot of things you wished you hadn't," I guess, keeping my voice soft, sympathetic.

Her eyes fill with fresh tears. "Yeah."

"Tell me." I sift my hand through her hair, releasing more of her scent. I don't want to drag her through bad memories, but I know she doesn't share much of herself with others. Maybe getting it out would help.

She shakes her head, shoulders slumping. "All kinds of things. Werewolves, for one thing." Her lips twist into a wry grimace.

"Yeah, I think we've covered that."

"I saw my high school English teacher's husband beating her up, the rape of a friend. I see people's traumas, their worst secrets. It's a fucking curse. I have a recurring dream of a puppy standing in blood." Tears fall down her face. "And every time I have it, someone dies. First my dad. Later, my mom. Then a social worker. When I was little, I thought I made it happen."

I slide my arm around her shoulders and pull her in close. "I'm sorry, sweetheart. That's terrible."

She sniffs. "Yeah. I only see bad things—" she breaks off, staring at me, her eyes wide, and all the air leaves the Range Rover.

"You think I'm a bad thing?" I guess, my organs turning to stone.

She swallows and studies the tattoo on my hand.

Maybe I am bad for her. Fuck. The fact that she knows about us puts her at risk from any vigilante pack member who gets nervous about her. The fact my wolf wants to mark her with his teeth puts her at risk of being shackled to me for her whole life or, worse, dying from infection or bleed-out.

But I'm not going to let anything bad happen to her. No matter what.

"You see secrets," I say firmly. "Shifting is mine. Doesn't mean I'm going to harm you, baby." Even as I speak, I doubt she will believe me. I strong-armed her into coming with me. I've kept her on edge to win her silence.

Her gaze drifts out the window of the car, her expression blank.

Damn. I fucked everything up.

6

___

Garrett

We arrive at the beach at sunset, pulling into Condos Pilar, the cluster of vacation rentals nestled along the white sand. I get out and stalk to the door of the condo where Sedona stayed, not waiting to see if the rest follow. I rap on the door and hear the voices of the young people and running footsteps.

"Hey man." Jason, the young kid who called, opens the door. The rest of the kids stare at me with pinched faces. I met them all when Sedona stopped by on her way out, but damn if I remember all their names. The place smells like sunscreen, liquor, and a sour smell that reminds me of nausea.

Trey, Jared, and Amber arrive behind me as the group of college students gather around. They repeat their stories, each a variation of what I already heard: Sedona went for a run on the beach that morning and never returned. No one saw anyone or anything menacing. They spoke with the authorities and filed a report, but since she hadn't been missing twenty-four hours, nothing was being done.

My fists tighten at my sides, wolf rages beneath the surface. The more they talk, the more I feel like I'm coming out of my skin. Finally, I reach for Amber. My wolf needs her close, and I'm willing to give him whatever he wants to keep from shifting and tearing this place apart. Already the kids look nervous, their gazes on the floor or darting to me, then away. Humans don't often understand animal dominance, but their primal brains recognize a predator when they see one.

Amber leans into me, her arm slipping around my waist and giving me a squeeze. She's still too pale, biting her lower lip. I scared her, bringing her down here and keeping her from escaping. But, here she is, comforting me. Her warm weight against my side keeps me focused.

"Okay, do you know how we can rent a place to stay here for the night?" I ask. It's almost dark, and I'm dying to shift and sniff the entirety of the beach.

"Actually, we were thinking we'd head back home tonight. We could go report it to the authorities in Tucson. So you could stay here."

Normally, I'd do anything to avoid involving the authorities, but, in this instance, not knowing what had happened to Sedona, I want all the help we can get. I should call my parents, too, but I don't want to worry my mom or my dad to start a war. If I can find Sedona first, it, would be better. If not, I'll call them in the morning. "That sounds like a good plan. Thank you all."

Within twenty minutes, Sedona's friends leave. We settle into the place, my pack mates searching the refrigerator to eat the leftovers from the college students.

"We'll go sniff the beach." Jared shucks his T-shirt.

I flex my muscles, my body itching to shift as well. While I trust Trey and Jared, my wolf won't rest until I've done the sniffing myself. But I can't leave Amber here alone. I'm not certain she'll stay put. Her attempt to climb out the bathroom window at the border crossing has me cautious.

"Bring me the duct tape from the trunk of the Range Rover," I order Trey in an undertone. He raises his brows like he thinks I'm nuts, but obeys.

When he returns, I take Amber's hand, leading her toward a bedroom.

Once inside, she turns. "Are you okay?"

"Yeah." I blow out a breath. I can't forget she betrayed us, no matter how much my wolf wants her. "Listen, baby. I need to go shift and sniff the beach. I'm really sorry about this." I spin her around and pin her wrists behind her back.

"What in the hell—stop it!" she shrieks, real panic entering her voice.

"Easy, easy," I murmur in her ear. While this is a necessity, I'm going for seductive rather than abusive. I'm hard as a rock, and I remember how much she liked being restrained last night. If I can keep it sexy, I just might pull this off without her hating me for the rest of our lives.

I work quickly, wrapping the duct tape around her wrists and picking her up by the waist. "You're safe with me, Counselor. Nothing terrible is going to happen. It's just that after that little escape stunt you pulled at the border, I don't feel comfortable leaving you here alone while I go check out the beach."

Amber's resistance slackens. I sense her confusion.

I nip the shell of her ear. "Be a good girl, and I promise I'll reward you when I get back, baby. I'll even keep you tied up."

"You sadistic—"

I cut her tirade off with a hard kiss.

When I break it, she looks at me dazedly, lips parted. Gritting my teeth to keep from prying those legs apart to reward her immediately, I restrain her, plunking her in a high-backed chair and pinning her there while I rip off tape. Little angry grunts escape her.

Sexy little grunts.

"You growling at me, princess?"

"Don't call me that!"

"You're so fucking cute when you're mad." I secure her wrists and tie her to the chair.

"Let me go, Garrett. This isn't funny."

I drop to my knees at her feet and pry her legs apart. She's wearing the yoga pants from this morning, and her arousal has leaked through. I press my face into the apex of her thighs, open my mouth, and nip at her sex through the thin fabric.

She thrusts her pussy toward my mouth, making the cutest sound of dissatisfaction. "We both know you like being restrained, Counselor." I stroke my thumb slowly over her slit. "I'll make it up to you when I get back. You have my word."

She looks so beautiful, eyes dilated, hair mussed, full lips parted. My wolf surges to the surface, and my vision domes. *Fuck.* I guess I still want to mark her. Desperately.

Time to leave.

I rip off another piece of tape and clamp it down on her mouth. "Sorry, sweetheart. But this is the only way I feel comfortable leaving you. Trey will be right in the living room if you need anything. I'll be back soon. No more than a couple hours."

"Rmphel mphs!" she repeats in a muffled scream.

"Be good." I stroke her hair, watching her tits jiggle as

she keeps squirming. "Are you hungry? Do you need anything before I go?"

Her brows slam together. "Mmm, mmm, mmm, mmm." She kicks at me, eyes narrowed.

"No? Okay, baby. Bathroom? I guess I should've asked that before I taped you up. No? All right. I'll be back before you know it."

I tug her head to the side and nip her neck. "Please don't wear yourself out fighting with that tape."

Another furious scream, and I can't stop myself leaning down to kiss her lips through the tape. She tries to head butt me.

Chuckling, I rear back and look her up and down. Her chest heaves, and there are pink spots on her cheeks. Fucking gorgeous. "This is a good look for you," I drawl, just to see the anger and frustration spark again in her eyes.

She stills, and glares at me. "Uck. Oo." She enunciates each word clearly, as best she can behind the tape.

"There's my good bad girl."

~.~

Amber

Let the record reflect: *I'm going to buy the biggest nutcracker in existence.* I'll see how Garrett McJerkwolf likes getting tied up when he has a silver ballbuster clamped to his nards.

First I have to get out of here.

I wrench at the tape for the thousandth time, but it won't budge.

The front door bangs open. I sit up straighter, ready to go another round with a werewolf. But when Garrett walks in, his head down, shoulders slumped, worry lines creasing his forehead, all the fight drains out of me. I don't need a vision to show me he found nothing.

He's shirtless. His sculpted pecs, lightly dusted with brown curls, stand out in relief above the eight-pack abs and narrow waist. The moment he sees me, the bar of his enormous cock presses against the front his jeans. I noticed it when he tied me up, too. The fact it made me crazy horny only pisses me off even more.

I make a questioning sound, eyebrows raised.

"Nothing." He shakes his head. "There's no sign of her. All three of us shifted, but I couldn't catch her scent. The ocean probably washed it away."

I make another comforting noise. He looks so dejected.

He pulls the tape from my mouth, and the sting helps me remember my rage.

"Ow," I snap.

"Sorry." He breaks the tape from my chest and wrists with his bare hands, ripping it from me like it's tissue paper.

"I have some things to tell you, buddy."

"I'm sure you do, Counselor." Looking tired, but amused, he folds his arms across his chest, mirroring me. For some reason, this sends my temper into the red zone.

"That's funny. You acting like you respect me. Because last time I checked, when you respect a woman, you don't kidnap her and drive her across the border to Mexico." I channel Lawyer Amber as hard as I can to keep from screaming like a crazy person. "You do realize this is the worst second date in the history of dating. And that's saying something because the first one was epically, epically bad. And—why are you grinning at me like that?"

"My wolf thinks you're adorable when you're mad. But

be careful, little lawyer. I'm real riled up right now. And I know just what would make me feel better."

"What?"

"Tossing you over my shoulder, carrying you to the bed, and fucking you six ways to Sunday,"

"It is almost Sunday." My voice sounds strangled. My lady bits are cheering.

"Nope." Garrett's grin is feral. "Not this Sunday. Next. It'll take about a week." He leans forward. "How's that end to our second date?"

"This isn't a date."

"I know. You're the one who called it that. You like spending time with me, Counselor?"

"What? No, I—" My cheeks flood. Damn my libido for picking this moment to go into overdrive.

Garrett steps close enough for me to feel his chuckle in my panties. "I promise our third date will be epically better."

"Look." I hold up a hand, trying to put space between us. It lands on his rock-hard chest, which doesn't help my focus at all. "Your sister is missing. We need to find her."

My reminder sucks the energy out of the room. *Damn.* So much for my reward. I should have let him keep me tied up a little longer.

"Yeah," Garrett sighs, and slumps. He looks about a thousand years old. "You saw her surrounded by men, so she didn't drown. Or get lost. She's been gone for twelve hours now. No human could have taken her—she'd rip their throat out. So it has to be other shifters."

"All right. You brought me here to help. How can I help?"

He stabs his fingers through his tousled blond hair. "Really?"

I nod. I hate being Crazy Amber, I'm afraid of becoming her, but I've never been the type of person to walk away from someone in need. If he thinks I can help, I have to help. Even if he did technically kidnap me and bind me with duct tape.

"Here's the thing. We're at the point I should call in my dad. But, if he comes down here, he's going to bring a hundred armed wolves and tear this town apart before asking questions. If you could get any more information before I call him down, it might keep wolves—particularly Sedona—from getting hurt."

"But I don't know how to use the visions. They just come."

He picks up my hand and rubs his thumb over the back of it. "Just try?"

"Okay," I whisper.

Crap. I am so not ready to embrace this side of myself. Especially around these people—*wolves*—I hardly know.

Except Garrett doesn't seem like a stranger. Not at all. And he doesn't make me feel crazy, either. Maybe I can do this.

I can at least try.

~.~

Garrett

"So, who do you think took Sedona?" Jared asks as we sit around the table eating the fish tacos he and Trey bought. It's late, but no one can sleep. "Did you see what they looked like in your, um, vision or whatever?"

Amber shakes her head. She leans against the kitchen counter, eating standing up. Still putting distance between us. It's a good idea, but I want to pull her into my lap and feed her with my fingers.

"Were they wolves?" Trey cranks his neck around to look at her.

Her brow wrinkles. "No, they were men—oh." She pauses. "Well, how would I know? Is there a telltale sign or something?"

"Their eyes. Did they change color, or glow?"

Frowning, she shakes her head. "I don't remember."

"Can you have the vision again?"

"It's not like a movie I rent. They just come to me."

"You don't control them at all?"

I frown at Trey to shut him up.

"No," she snaps. "That's not the way they work."

"Well, that sucks," Trey mumbles.

I growl, and he adjusts his expression to something friendlier.

"Look, I'm trying." Amber sets down her food and turns to the sink. She spends about a minute washing her hands, then grabs a paper towel and starts wiping down the counters.

"Hey." I push out of my chair, and amble over to her. I don't mean to crowd her, but she drops the paper towel and backs up anyway. "We're all just trying to figure this psychic thing out."

She flinches at the word *psychic*. "You don't understand. I've spent my entire life suppressing these visions."

"Is that why you get headaches?"

Her shoulders lift and fall.

"Have you ever tried just letting them happen?"

"I can't."

I tilt my head to the side.

"I've never tried," she amends. "I'm afraid they'll take over my life."

"Okay. May I try something?"

"Like what?" She watches me warily. She used to trust me, against her better judgment. But I broke it. This distance between us? It's my fault.

"I'm going to touch you," I murmur.

Behind me, Jared clears his throat.

"Please," I add.

A small hesitation, and she nods.

"Just breathe. Relax."

I place a hand over her eyes. "Close your eyes." Her lashes flutter against my palm. "Just feel into it. Humans or wolves?"

She stays quiet for so long, I give up on an answer. The heat of her body, so close to mine, makes my cock thicken. I breathe in her scent, knowing I should back away, keep my hands off her if I want to maintain control.

"Wolves," she says at last.

I force myself to step back. "I knew it."

"What do you think they want with her?" Jared asks. He and Trey come to their feet.

I run my fingers through my hair. "Probably breeding."

Amber looks shocked, so I explain. "Many shifters consider our species endangered. Our DNA has been diluted too much with human genes. It's considered a sin against our kind to mate with a human. But that means in smaller communities in-breeding is now the problem."

"What happens when they mate with a human?" Amber asks.

"These days, they produce human babies." I meet her intelligent gaze. Is she thinking about what might happen if we continue on the path we're on, this doomed dance of attraction? "Offspring who never get sick and heal quickly, but human, not wolf."

"They can't shift?"

"Right. I mean, there are half-breeds who shift—it's not unheard of. There's a panther in Tucson who didn't shift until she got pregnant with a wolf shifter's pup. But it's rare."

"So you think they spot a female wolf who hasn't been part of their pack, and just grab her for breeding?" Amber's voice sharpens, and I get a hint of what she must be like on crusade.

I bet she's fucking amazing in the courtroom. I get hard just picturing her in one of her fitted suits, pacing the room in high heels, dazzling every male in the building with those shapely calves, that sharp mind.

"I think it's possible, yeah. She's an alpha female, and young enough to bear lots of pups."

Amber swallows, looking a little sick. "We have to get her back."

"Yeah." My stomach clenches. "Soon. Before they start..." I can't finish the sentence. My fists tighten, itching to punch someone. My wolf wants to rampage. I want to break everything I see. If Amber weren't here, I probably already would have.

"So what do we do?" she asks, chin up like she's ready to do anything. She's not going to like what we have to do.

"We have no leads, Amber. No scent at all. We got nothing but your vision. Let's play twenty questions with you and see what you can intuit."

Her shoulders slump. Doubt oozes from her stance. I step so my body blocks my two packmates watching her, and cup her chin. "You can do this, Amber. Your gifts are meant to be used."

"What if I'm wrong? Or I can't see anything?"

"It will still be more information than we have now."

"You're crazy," she mutters, but she walks to the couch and sits down, tucking her legs up under her body and closing her eyes. "Go ahead."

Trey has his laptop open. "It says here that psychics can be clairsentient, clairvoyant, clairaudient or claircognizant. Which do you think you are, Amber?"

"Clairvoyant. I see things--I don't usually hear. Maybe clairsentient--sometimes I feel things like emotion. Especially his." She shifts her gaze to me.

"G, do you have something of Sedona's?" Trey asks. "It says that police psychics hold an object that belonged to a victim or missing person to kick start the intuition."

I go to the room Sedona stayed in and grab one of her tank tops from her suitcase. I hand it to Amber. "This belongs to Sedona."

"Can't hurt to try, I guess," Amber mumbles, taking the shirt and holding it in both hands. She closes her eyes.

"Where is Sedona now?"

Amber sits perfectly still while three pairs of eyes stare at her in silence. Minutes tick by. She exhales in a whoosh as if she's been holding it. "I don't know," she says at last.

"Is she in San Carlos still?"

Another long pause and then a shake of her head. "Sorry."

"Can you get a name of one of the men who took her?"

Agitation radiates from my little human, but she squeezes her eyes shut again. "La...Luh...Lobo?" Her eyes snap open. "Oh, that's stupid. That's just *wolf* in Spanish."

"No, you may be onto something. It could be the last name of a family of wolves."

"Your father might have contacts with some of the packs down here," Jared says in a low voice.

I blow out a breath. I was hoping to find my sister fast, without involving my dad. "First, let's do some digging. We need a lead." I know my dad. He'll drive down with every warrior wolf in his pack, maybe even from packs who owe him favors. It'll be war. My gut tells me Sedona will pay the price.

We've gotta get more information. "Trey? Will you see if Kylie can help with research?"

One of the shifters in Tucson—the panther who mated a wolf—is a tech genius. She can hack any system in the world for information.

"I'm on it," Trey says.

"Is she in a house right now? Outside? Is she in wolf form or human?" Jared asks.

Amber's face pinches, and she shakes her head. "I'm sorry, you guys. I just don't know." She looks pale and exhausted. My wolf whines, hating her distress.

"Okay," I say. "Amber, why don't you get some rest? It's been a long day. We'll try again in the morning."

"No, that's okay, I can keep going. Ask another one."

"Amber." I start to put an alpha-push to my voice. Jared catches my eye, and I back down. "All right. One more."

"What step should we take next to find her?" Jared asks.

"Hmm, interesting question." Amber closes her eyes again as Trey walks outside to call Kylie. I motion for Jared to follow him.

I sit back down and wait in silence, the sound of the waves crashing on the beach outside making a lullaby to ease the tension in the room. Amber gives a soft sigh. She's fallen asleep.

As tight as my gut is right now, as much as I want to find Sedona, I can't bear to wake Amber. I lift her carefully. Her eyelids flutter, but she doesn't open them. Her lips move, but I don't catch what she's saying.

"What's that?"

She furrows her brow and shakes her head. "I don't know."

"Yes, you do. You know," I assure her, carrying her into the bedroom. How can she have gone this long without anyone telling her how powerful and special her talent really is? A gift, not the curse she believes it to be.

I pull back the covers and lay her on the bed. My little spitfire looks so fragile asleep, the line between her brows creased with worry. My wolf is calmer now, and I can't resist brushing a kiss on that little line. If she were my mate, I'd do everything I could to make sure she never had cause to worry again.

~.~

Amber

I wake to find myself on the bed in the bedroom, Garrett sitting in the chair, chin in hand and eyes on me.

"How long was I out?" I croak.

"An hour. Any headaches?"

"No. Watching over your prisoner?" I murmur, sitting up and rubbing my eyes. I stretch my arms over my head, arching my back. Was the previous sizzling attraction a fluke?

Nope. I spy with my little eye something that begins with C, growing long and hard against his jeans.

"You take this kidnapping thing seriously." I really

shouldn't poke the bear...wolf...but I can't help it. He looks so delicious with his dark scruff and tousled hair.

"I could've tied you up again." His voice is deeper than usual, his eyes boiling.

My pussy clenches, but I school my face. He doesn't need to know how well he plays the game.

His nostrils flare, his eyes turning silver as he sniffs the air. "You're close to ovulation."

"What?" I yank the covers up, thankful I'm still fully clothed.

"You cycle with the moon. Not many human females do, anymore."

I glance at the window, where the curtains frame a full moon.

"Two days," he answers my silent question. His pewter gaze makes me pull the covers up under my chin.

So, what happens during the full moon?

I go hunting.

"What does that mean to you?" I ask.

"I might have to lock you up to keep you safe." His glittering gaze screams *big bad wolf.*

"You already did that."

"I mean lock you away from me."

Lust kicks through me. Garrett leans forward, his hands clenched together, his tattoos clear.

He's a menace, I remind myself. *He kidnapped you. Tied you up.*

A pulse grows between my legs. It would be so easy to push the covers back down, spread my legs. Play with myself. See how long it takes him to lose control.

No, no, no. Bad girl.

This guy is every bad decision I never made, rolled into

one. And if I don't snap out of lust soon, I'm going to make what might be the biggest mistake of my life.

A knock sounds on the bedroom door.

"Hey, boss?" Jared calls.

"Yeah," Garrett gives his head a quick, dog-like shake and unfolds from the chair. He prowls to the door with a smooth speed, silent as a wolf. As a predator.

"I heard back from Kylie. She sent the list of people with the last name 'Lobo' in the surrounding area, and then all of Mexico. There's one nearby. We'll drive over and sniff around right now."

"Thanks, guys," Garrett says. "I'll stay here and pick Amber's brain."

I bite my lip as the guys leave. A woman is missing. Whatever Garrett and I have for each other, it can wait.

Thirty minutes later, I'm pacing the living room, balling my hands into fists. "I don't know. I just don't know. I wish I could help, but I can't."

"Just relax. You're too wound up. Lie down on the sofa and close your eyes."

My stomach twists up in a double-knot. "I can't. Garrett, this isn't working. I'm not going to be able to help you. You've got to find another way."

"It is working. It has worked. I'm just asking you to try again."

"For God's sake, I can't," I snap, then close my mouth when I see pain on his face. I force myself to exhale. "I'm sorry, but you're stressing me out. This whole experience is very intense."

"I know. That's why I wanted you to sit down. You need to relax. Either figure out how to do it for yourself, or I'll help you."

Excuse me? I whirl, my hands on my hips. "You'll help

me? Exactly how do you plan to do—" I stop speaking when Garrett stalks toward me, pulling his T-shirt off over his head.

I back up, even though my ovaries rev their engines.

You're close to ovulation. Who says that? A werewolf, I suppose.

"Wh-what are you doing?"

His lips twist in a wry grin. "I know what helps me relax..."

"Oh no." I dart to the side to avoid his grasp.

He moves shockingly fast for a man his size, snatching me up by the waist and swinging me around as I kick uselessly. "What did I tell you about running from a wolf?" he growls, his breath hot against my ear.

"Stop it! Put me—" I gasp when he rubs the seam of my yoga pants roughly against my clit. My pussy spasms with pleasure.

"You know you want this." The rumble of his words reverberate from his chest right to my core. "You've known since the first night we met it's an inevitability."

I lean my head back against him. "No, I don't," I lie, a giggle leaving my throat as I thrash. I don't even know why I fight him, except out of indignation at his cocksure certainty.

"Oh yes you do. You think I can't smell every time your pussy gets wet for me?"

I go still, contemplating that. How many times have I been wet for him since the day we met? And he's known? *Every time?* Eek.

I close my mouth on a moan as he continues to thrill my pussy with his rough pawing through my yoga pants.

"You can keep lying to me and yourself, but this respon-sive little body of yours always tells the truth." He manages to pin me back against his chest and slide a hand up my shirt, his palm cupping my breast and squeezing.

I arch with a cry of pleasure.

He pinches the stiffened bud of my nipple between his fingers and rolls it, while the digits of his other hand continue to pulse against my clit, grinding the seam of my pants against it. "Did you think I missed every time these little nipples got hard, or the way your eyes dilate when you're thinking about what would happen if—no, *when*, you're finally claimed by the big bad wolf?"

My first mini-orgasm shoots through me, a shudder he surely feels. So much for pretending I don't want it.

He bends his knee and brings it up between my legs, holding my weight while he moves, freeing both hands to grasp the waistband of my pants.

"Don't," I squeak, but my voice sounds far more wanton than serious.

"Say yes," he murmurs in my ear.

"I'm not...I don't..." I moan at the sheer pleasure he's eliciting in my nether regions.

"You need it."

He slides the flat of his hand down the front of my pants and cups my mound. I jerk the moment his hot fingers touch my wet pussy, and I wrap my hand around behind myself to hold his neck.

He slows down, tilting me back on his knee and running one digit up and down the length of my weeping slit. "Say yes," he murmurs. He bites my ear. "And I'll let you come."

"*Let* me come?"

No one *lets* me come. I come when I...my eyes roll back in my head as his thick fingers part my labia and explore my inner pleats. Jesus, his index finger is as thick as some men's cocks. I want it inside me.

As if reading my mind, he slides it in, alone, first, then with his middle finger, filling and stretching me, stroking the inside of my wanton pussy.

I claw the back of his neck, fighting like a cat in heat, which he doesn't seem to mind.

"That's right, princess. *Let* you come." He abruptly removes his digits and taps my clit lightly. "Or do you want me to leave you all wound up like this?"

"I-I could finish on my own." Technically, it's true. Although it wouldn't be half so satisfying.

He lowers his knee, dropping my feet to the floor.

"Yes," I bark in a hurry, all pride dissolving when faced with the loss of his hot hands on my body. "I said *yes*."

He chuckles and picks me up. "Good girl," he murmurs in my ear as he carries me to the bedroom and tosses me onto the bed like a rag doll.

I prop myself on my elbows, watching him crawl up over me, his cock bulging against his jeans, his expression ravenous. "I'm going to make you come so hard you scream."

Arrogant much? But then, he probably has reason to be confident. A man—or wolf—whatever, who looks like him probably has girls throwing themselves at him on a regular basis.

He grabs my pants on either side and yanks them down, tearing my panties off in the process and throwing them both over his shoulder. Grasping my knees, he parts them and bends them up, opening me to him. "I did promise you a reward."

I gasp at the shock of vulnerability, of having my most intimate parts spread and displayed for his close inspection. He brings the pad of his thumb to my clit, just rests it there, as if he knows I need a moment to calm down and get used to his touch.

"Lace your fingers together behind your head."

I stare at him, my brain slow to process his words. When he arches a stern brow, I force my mind to replay his words and bring my hands out of the way. The position increases my sense of exposure, but I immediately forget when Garrett brings the tip of his tongue to the seam of my labia, parting the lips and running along the inside of each before circling my clit. Already on fire, I jerk at the touch, bucking.

He holds my pelvis down with one huge hand and penetrates me with his tongue, his thumb returning to my engorged clit and gently vibrating.

I lose my breath in a cry, hands flying down to push his head away, the sensation too much.

"Uh uh," he scolds, abruptly stopping all his ministrations. "What did I tell you about your hands?"

"I'm sorry," I whimper, desperate for him to go on—as desperate as I'd been for him to stop a moment before.

He pulls his knees up underneath him and sits up, grabbing my ankles and lifting them into the air.

"What are you— Ow!"

Garrett transfers both my ankles to one hand and slaps my ass with the other one—hard. He rubs away the sting then lands another one and another. They aren't gentle, light spanks, but hard and deliberate, catching my bulging labia and exposed sex with each slap, his palm coming away wet with my juices. The fire he ignites is more than surface sting; it comes from my very core.

Even so, I fight him, kick my legs, though they barely move in his grasp.

It's horrible and incredible at once. I'm helpless, but, for once in my life, I'm not fighting for control. I let him have it. Let him punish me because I know what's coming next.

Pleasure.

Pure, unadulterated pleasure.

"Little girls who disobey get punished, don't they baby?" I hear pure sex in his voice, and I moan in response. "What's that, angel?"

"Yes, sir." I don't even know what makes me say it. It's not like I watch BDSM porn or know anything about being spanked by a lover, but it just comes out.

He growls, eyes turning silver. "Oh, baby. You have me harder than stone."

As I writhe and wriggle under the onslaught of his hand, I'm suddenly desperate to help him with his harder-than-stone cock. How much would fit in my mouth?

He stops spanking, and I let out a soft, low moan. He lifts my ankles even higher in the air and plants a kiss on each raw cheek before lowering my pelvis.

I tuck my hands underneath, cupping my hot, tingling buttocks, still panting from the punishment. Of their own accord, my knees part and pelvis lifts in offering.

He chuckles. "What are we going to do about these hands?"

I immediately snatch them away, my ass giving a reminder pulse of what happens when I disobey. I both want and don't want more of the same. "Sorry, sir."

~.~

Garrett

Oh no.

She did not just call me *sir* again. Fates, she's testing my self-control.

My cock punches out against my jeans, painfully hard

and dying to plow into Amber. But I'm not going to. No, this is for her. I owe her pleasure. Besides, I don't trust myself with her.

"I'm tempted to tie you up, since you're having a hard time following directions, but I don't want to get kicked in the nuts, which I strongly suspect would happen if I tried it again."

She gives a short bark of laughter. "I *was* thinking about acquiring some silver nutcrackers."

I lower myself and return to my earlier pleasure, tasting her incredible pussy. I lick into her, nipping her lips with my teeth. "Baby. you taste so good to me."

She jerks. "Oh God!"

I lift the hood of her clit and flick it with my tongue then suck the little nub until her legs thrash around my ears and her choked breath sounds desperate. I thrust two fingers inside her sopping channel and swirl them around, stroking her inner walls. Finding her G-spot, I tickle it, feeling the tissue harden under my fingertips as her voice turns to a screech.

I lick the thumb of my other hand for lubrication and wiggle it between her butt cheeks, seeking her little rosette. Her pelvis pops up from the bed, but I follow her movements, circling the tight ring of muscle, pressing into it.

"Stop... what? Oh God," she squeals.

I shove my thumb in and out of her ass as I continue to stroke her G-spot. I don't stop fucking her, filling both her holes, demanding more and more of her. My vision has domed, my wolf is growling, but I'll be damned if I'm going to give him an inch. This isn't about me putting my cock in a hot human, not even one my wolf has attached himself to. I fight the urge to swap my fingers for my cock, to pound her sweet pussy until we both shatter.

Amber's already close, so close.

"Come for me, baby," I growl. "Come all over my fingers now."

She lasts only three seconds longer. She explodes, screaming as I promised, bucking and kicking, her internal muscles tightening and spasming around my fingers as she unravels in the most gorgeous display of an orgasm I've ever seen.

I keep pumping until she collapses into a lifeless heap, then I ease my fingers out and plant a kiss on the swollen lips of her sweet little pussy. "I'll be right back." I scramble up and get myself into the bathroom to wash up and get my wolf under control.

This was for Amber. *Not* for me.

But my wolf doesn't give a fuck about whatever decision I've made not to claim Amber. He's pissed I still have a full cock and an unmated female.

I force myself to think about Sedona and, after a few breaths, he backs down. I was relaxing Amber so she can help Sedona. Not mating her.

Once I'm calm, I return and find she hasn't moved, her legs sprawled open, arms flung wide. Her mussed hair and flushed cheeks make her look thoroughly fucked. *By me*. My wolf preens. I climb over her and kiss her neck, settling beside her.

"What about you?" she asks hoarsely.

"I don't think you're ready for wolf cock," I joke, hoping I've hidden my grimace of pain. I seriously think I might die if I don't fuck her brains out soon. But Amber's not mine for the taking. I have no plans to mate any female, especially not a human. And, damn, but I don't think I'm capable of just fooling around with her. Not with my wolf howling at me to mark her.

"No?" she pouts. She's adorable. Her armor's fallen away, and I get to see the real Amber underneath. The sweet, soft, angelic Amber. And fates, if I'm not careful, I'm going to hurt her, despite my best intentions. I need to tell her we can't do this. Now.

She gets up onto her hands and knees and crawls toward me. It's pure sex-slave stuff, and I almost pass out just watching. She flicks open the button on my jeans.

I grab her hands to stop her, but it's too late. She brings that hot, moist mouth to my cock and bites through my boxer briefs.

"Fuck." I grab her by the hair and hold her mouth still with one hand, whipping out my cock with the other.

She opens wide.

Ah fates, I shouldn't. I really shouldn't. But I can't seem to pull back. I plunge deep into her mouth, bumping the back of her throat and making her gag. I immediately pull back, shocked at what an asshole I am. "I told you you can't handle wolf cock," I say, but it comes out strangled.

"Oh yeah?" Yeah, my girl loves a challenge because she's immediately back on my cock, sucking hard as she draws it into the pocket of her cheek and out. She grips the base and strokes her hand up and down in synchronized movements with her mouth, making it seem like she's taking my full length.

My vision domes. My teeth elongate to mark her. I take a page out of the play I just made her follow and lace my fingers on the top of my head. I can't touch or I swear I'll throw her down and fuck the living daylights out of her. She looks so fucking hot, those full lips stretched around my throbbing cock, eyes trained on my face like the perfect submissive.

"Fates, Amber. I'll never say you can't handle wolf cock

again," I choke. I want to grab her head and urge her faster, but I don't let myself.

No touching.

Do not touch her if you want to keep her safe.

She picks up speed on her own, probably sensing how close I am from the way my thighs shake.

"Fuck, baby, I'm going to come," I growl. I start to pull out, but she doesn't let me. She grips my cock tighter in her little fist and sucks so damn hard.

Lights explode behind my eyes. I bellow, and the sound is more animal than human. I come in her mouth, and she sucks it down, swallows.

The release gives me a few precious seconds to get away from her. To keep from nailing that hot little pussy from here into eternity.

I lurch away and walk until I hit the door, where I shove my cock back in my pants and zip them up. I force myself to remain facing the door, like a kid in a timeout. Despite my orgasm, my flesh is still on fire, teeth still at the ready. I work to slow my breath. I can do this. I am an alpha wolf. If I don't have the self-discipline to master my beast, I don't deserve the position.

"Listen, Amber," I say in a strangled voice. "What we are... what we just did..."

"No, I know," she interrupts, getting up and putting her clothes on. "This was just to relax me." I dare to turn and see the soft happiness in her face disappear, like a light switched off.

The pain of that sight is enough for my wolf to pull way back. My vision clears. The teeth return to normal.

"We can't work long term." The words are heavy on my tongue. "Humans and... we don't work out long term. Believe me, baby, I want you. I want you so badly it hurts."

I grab my cock in my jeans for emphasis. "But I can't do it."

"You made your case," she says stiffly. "I'll stop thinking of this as our second date."

A terrible weight drops onto my chest. "No, it's definitely a date. I don't kidnap and duct tape just any girl, you know." I try for humor then sober again. "I want you to know, I don't do this"—I wave a hand to indicate the bed —"casually."

"Yeah right. I bet all those girls at the club throw themselves at you."

Do I detect a note of jealousy? My ego is momentarily cheered. "I don't," I growl.

She turns away from me as she steps into her yoga pants.

Fuck. I've hurt her. I definitely screwed this up. I walk up behind her and wrap an arm around her waist, but she stiffens. Sensing the walls she's erected kills me.

She picks up Sedona's tank like she's going to put it on instead of her shirt. Then she goes still.

I remain still, too, though I know my touch is unwelcome. It's like I need the physical closeness to try to counteract the chasm I've just put between us.

"She's in a cage, being taken out of an airplane and put in a white van."

I drop my hold on her and whirl her around. "Where?" I bark, cursing inwardly when she flinches.

"I don't know. The men handling her look Latino. So. maybe still in Mexico?"

"Where? What city?"

"I don't know."

I pause at the door, then stride back, catching Amber around the waist and pulling her close for a kiss. "Thank you."

She blushes. "Well, I don't know if it—"

I stop her protests with another kiss. "Thank you." I release her as abruptly as I snatched her up.

"Trey," I shout, slamming the bedroom door open. I'd heard the guys return a few minutes ago. "Call Kylie. Find out about every plane that left this area since Sedona disappeared—especially ones that might have been carrying a caged wolf."

The pierced wolf has his phone to his ear before I finish. "Closest airport is in Hermosillo."

I turn to Jared next. "Pull up a map of Mexico." When the tattooed wolf walks over with his laptop and the map on the screen, I bring it to Amber, who has dressed and come out of the bedroom. "Where?"

She gives me a doubtful look but gazes at the map.

"Don't think, just say the first thing that comes to your mind."

"Mexico City," she blurts, and then looks surprised, as if she didn't know she was going to speak. She blinks several times. "But I also heard the word *Lobo* again."

"I'll get Kylie to cross reference that area with the word *Lobo*," Trey says.

"Do it in the car." I nod to Jared, who starts packing up his laptop. "We need to get to Hermosillo."

7

Garrett

At daybreak the next morning, we get on a plane in Hermosillo. It's a direct flight to Mexico City. Three hours. I should have called my dad before we left. It's been almost twenty-four hours since Sedona disappeared, but there's some part of me that needs to handle this on my own. Prove I'm capable of leading my own pack, keeping my sister safe.

Hopefully, I'm not putting Sedona at more risk by waiting to call him.

I stare at the golden head resting on my shoulder, the shiny waves cascading down Amber's sleeping frame. She normally has her hair up, confined, out of reach. She holds back her trust the same way.

I finger a strand, rubbing the impossibly silky hair between my fingers.

Mine.

God, I want this little human. Not just to fuck, although that, too—definitely that. But my need for her goes beyond sex. I want to possess all of her—heart, body, soul. I want to mark her as my own. I want to treasure and spoil her, tell her every day how special she is. Guard and protect her so she can let her walls down and let her gift out. Live free.

But it's not in my genetic makeup to settle down. Besides, it's not possible. I can't have her and remain alpha, and my wolf is too dominant to be anything else.

I could pull up roots and live as a lone wolf, but I was raised in a pack, destined to lead one. My wolf is too social to be an outcast. The scorn of the pack and disappointment of my parents would be too much to bear. Even with Amber as my mate, my wolf might come to resent her for what I had to give up to claim her.

It's time for me to own up to my responsibilities and follow the rules.

Rule number one: *Humans and werewolves don't mix.*

The plane descends. Amber stirs, lifting her head from my shoulder and blinking as she takes my fingers and squeezes.

She lifts her face to me, about to say something, but I cut her off with a kiss. Cupping the back of her head, I stroke her lips with mine, taking my mind off my gnawing dread about Sedona with the best distraction ever. I lick into her mouth, sucking her tongue, biting at her lips. She tastes as sweet as she smells.

The plane bumps the ground, and I tear myself away. Time to focus.

I'm tense as we ride in the cab through thick afternoon traffic. Not even Amber's hand on my thigh calms me.

When we get to the closest hotel, Jared steps up to handle check-in. I wait with my back to the wall, where no one can surprise me. Humans look at me and then away, scuttling to give me space.

"Boss," Trey says softly, and I realize I'm growling, a soft, low sound that nonetheless intimidates everyone in a hundred foot radius.

As soon as we set foot in the hotel room, I almost turn around. "I can't do this." My voice chokes with my wolf. "I can't be closed up."

"All right," Amber says. "Let's go look around."

I nod, chest heaving in an effort to get control. "I would if I knew where to go. Anything from Kylie yet?"

"No. Oh wait—it just came in. Here"—Trey holds up his phone—"Kylie found the name of the passenger traveling with a canine on the plane leaving Hermosillo last night. He's a textile importer with a warehouse here. I've got the address."

A growl rips out of me at full volume. Trey staggers back a little, showing his throat.

"Garrett," Amber touches my arm, as my vision tunnels.

I'm about to go under.

"You have to keep control. Sedona needs you."

"Stay," I grit out.

She nods. "I'll stay here. Will you leave me a phone? Mine doesn't have service here."

I check my phone to make sure it works and toss it on the dresser. "Trey and Jared's numbers are in there."

"Boss? When are we going to tell the rest of the pack?"

"We go now, scout out. See if she's there and if we can get her out. If we need reinforcements, I'll call in my dad. He'll bring both packs, and it will mean war."

~.~

Amber

I pace the length of the hotel room. I ordered room service, but I can't eat the *torta*—a toasted Mexican sandwich, filled with ham and cheese.

I find myself toying with my hair, and twist it up into a bun, only to yank it down several minutes later. I'm coming apart at the seams.

Crazy Amber.

To pull back Lawyer Amber, I file imaginary civil lawsuits against the men who captured Sedona. List all the ways I could bring them down.

But what if Garrett's right? What if Crazy Amber is the only one who can save her?

Not crazy.

Garrett thinks my visions are a gift.

I sit cross-legged on the bed. "Come to me," I breathe, trying to call up the relaxed state I had with Garrett. Immediately, my cheeks heat. I shift on my bottom, ignoring the tickle in my special spot. I hope I don't have to masturbate or receive servicing from a hulking wolf-man every time I need a vision. I let out a humorless laugh. I need to stop this attachment to Garrett. There's nothing for us, no future. He made that plain.

Find Sedona. In this, at least, I can help him.

Where is Garrett now?

Pain stabs my head. Fuck. Does that mean I'm holding back my inner sight? I get up and pace around the room. Seeing Garrett's bag, I rummage through it and pull out one of his shirts.

"Give it to me," I call out like an absolute madwoman.

Instantly, visions flood my head. Wolves in cages lined

up next to one another—dozens of them. One of them, a giant gray wolf, throws himself against the bars, growling.

I come out of my vision, heaving, and throw my hands out to steady myself. My body is charged and ready with adrenaline, as if I had been in one of those cages.

Garrett? I ask. Was that Garrett in the cage?

Urgency throws me off the bed. But what should I do? Another vision swims into focus, and I close my eyes. Garrett leans against my door back in Tucson, showing me how to pick a lock.

I open my eyes. The clock shows six p.m. Precious time lost.

I know what I have to do.

~.~

Amber

A half hour later, the cab I hailed pulls up one block away from the warehouse.

Mouth dry, I pay the cabbie and start walking. Dusk presses upon the concrete buildings; litter scatters in the street. Graffiti covers several of the buildings. The warehouse in question, though, has a fresh paint job and tall, electric fences.

I hesitate.

What if this doesn't end well? Who will help Sedona?

I pull out Garrett's phone, which I snagged from the dresser in the hotel before I left. Scroll through his contacts to one called *Dad*

I punch it.

A deep voice that sounded remarkably similar to Garrett's answered. "Hi, Son."

"Hi Mr. Green. My name is Amber Drake, I'm a, uh, friend of your son?"

"What's going on, Amber?" Power vibrates through the phone, and I almost drop it. Garrett wasn't kidding when he talked about alpha dominance.

"Sedona was kidnapped, and Garrett, Trey, Jared, and I followed her down to Mexico City. Garrett and the guys went to a warehouse, but I believe they've been captured as well. I'm outside, ready to go in and rescue them, but had to call someone and tell them what was happening first."

"Who are you?"

"I'm Garrett's neighbor."

There was a pause, and I knew what he wanted to ask. "Human, yes." *Psychic.* I still can't say it. "Garrett planned to call you if he needed reinforcements. If you don't hear from me or Garrett in the next few hours, you need to come and bring both packs."

"I will be on a plane tonight with reinforcements. You sit tight until we get there."

"I'm already at the warehouse. I'm going in."

"*No.* Stay where you are until I get there." Clearly, the elder wolf is as bossy and protective as his son. "You will not go in alone. Wait until I arrive."

"I'm sorry, Mr. Green, but I have to go, I'm already here. I just wanted to get you the address in case I don't return. I'll text it."

"No, dammit—"

I end the call and silence the phone. It flashes with *Dad* again, immediately, while I text the address to the warehouse, but I ignore the call and drop the device in my pocket. Before I lose my nerve, I force myself to cross the street and head towards the warehouse. I might be crazy, but it's what the situation calls for.

I open my mind to my intuition as I approach the forbidding concrete building. It hits me with a wave of nausea. My entire body shudders.

Which door? I ask, and let my attention drift. *Left of the building.*

Striding toward the door on that side, I scan the eaves for cameras. I don't know what to look for, but it appears clear.

I pull out the tools Garrett dropped in my purse the night he taught me to pick locks, take a deep breath, and imagine I'm back outside my apartment, Garrett's comforting bulk at my back.

Slow and steady, Counselor.

I hear a noise and drop the pick. Crouching, I wait. Spanish words and the smell of cigarette smoke waft my way. I grab the knob to pull myself up, and it turns. I almost laugh out loud. My intuition brought me to a entry that wasn't locked.

Inside, a long, dark hallway stretches ahead. Male voices come from a lighted room halfway down, along with the murmur of a television. If I go down the hall, I'll have to walk right past it.

I force myself to move, creeping like a wolf. Turns out the light in the hall comes from a window in the door. I duck under it and run the rest of the way down the hall. It dead ends into another entryway. I try the knob. *Locked.*

Fumbling in the dark, I palm the tools and insert them.

You can do it. I imagine Garrett's large hand closing over mine, guiding me.

Click. First tooth down. I hold it in place and press the second, then third, and ease the door open. Metal shelves house rows of cages. Most are empty, but four are occupied by enormous wolves.

Growls greet me. I slip inside and shut the door quickly, telling my heart to calm down. I'm in the wolf den, now. My basic instincts scream at me to turn and run from the roar of wild animals captive in this cavernous space. The warehouse must be soundproofed because I heard none of this outside.

Eyes glow and fangs snap at me as I go by. Which one is Garrett? I look for the large gray wolf from my vision. I don't see any white wolves, which means Sedona's not here.

I edge closer to a silver wolf in a cage but hesitate. Its eyes are yellow. Garrett's eyes turn silver.

I hear a horrible snarling to my left and whirl. An enormous silver-gray wolf throws himself against his cage, snapping and snarling.

"G-Garrett?"

The wolf launches at its cage, slamming his shoulder into the wires. Silver eyes. I recoil from the snapping jaws and gleaming teeth. It can't be Garrett; he wouldn't try to attack me. Except, I recognize those eyes. I know it's him.

I try to think rationally but can't bring myself to step any closer. This giant, terrifying animal snapping at the bars has no humanity.

"Garrett?" I try again.

A croak from several cages down reaches me. "It's him. He's freaking out because you're in danger." I identify the voice. Down the row, a naked human form curls in a cage. Jared.

"Is it safe to let him out?" I ask, my spine unraveling as Garrett snarls again.

"I don't know." Jared's face contorts in pain. He throws

his head back, his human form swallowed by an explosion of fur. Seconds later, a wolf stares at me.

Garrett's wolf lets out a half growl, half roar, and Jared's wolf whimpers and tucks tail. Goose bumps rise on my arms.

"All right," I whisper, and crouch so my head is lower than Garrett's wolf. "Hey, it's me. Amber."

My hands shake as I reach for the lock. He's right there, though, snarling through the bars at me.

"Would you mind backing off a bit? You're scaring me."

He throws his shoulder against the gate of the cage again.

"I need you to calm down, or I won't be able to concentrate. We have to get out of here so you can find Sedona, remember?"

Another half roar, and I cringe on the ground. Maybe mentioning his sister wasn't a good idea. Garrett's wolf paces back and forth, stopping to gnaw on the silver bars and bellow in pain.

I resist curling into a ball and pulling my shirt over my head like a child hiding from a monster. At any moment, Garrett's captors could come back here and find me. Then I'll be in a cage, too. If I'm lucky.

"We need to get out of here. Let me help you," I plead, careful not to make eye contact. Garrett's wolf chuffs but refuses to back away as I start to use the tools. His stare makes the hair on the back of my neck rise as I fiddle with the padlock.

As soon as I open the gate, Garrett launches out. I drop to the floor. He hurtles over my head, landing on all fours in a so-fast-he's-a-blur move that nearly makes me pee my pants. The giant wolf sniffs me up and down. I close my eyes, stifling a whimper. A satisfied chuff blows my hair back, and when I open my eyes, he's moved on. I guess he decided not to eat me. He lopes to the hallway and stops in front of it, growling.

"Okay, just a minute." I run to Jared's cage to spring the lock. The gray wolf, smaller than Garrett, is still frightening. One snap of those ferocious jaws, and I'll lose a limb.

Once he's out, he catches my purse strap in his teeth and tugs me to a third cage.

"Trey?" The gray-and-brown wolf licks my fingers through the cage as I fumble with the lock.

Garrett growls from the door again, and I rush to open it for him. With a furious roar, he and Trey barrel down the hall, towards the office.

"*Senorita*," a voice calls from a cage. "*Sueltame y te ayudaré.*" The cage of the yellow-eyed wolf now holds a naked man, whose black-eyed stare is no less intimidating than his wolf's.

Jared tugs my purse strap, but I resist.

"He says if I set him free, he will help us," I tell Jared, who stills as if considering. He cocks his head at me.

"I think we can trust him." My intuition comes as a warm feeling in my gut this time.

Guns fire down the corridor. I scream, dropping to the floor and scrambling back. Jared thrusts his body between me and the entryway. A grunt of pain, and he shifts again to human form.

I reach out a hand but don't touch him. Muscles ripple under his tattoos. He stands, and I keep my gaze on his face, but not before I notice taut six-pack abs etched into his tanned skin.

More shots blast through the hall.

"We need to help them," I cry, but Jared catches me before I can run forward.

"I don't think so, Counselor. Garrett would kill me if I left you unprotected."

"We have to do something."

"I—help," the strange wolf offers again.

"Give me the lock pick." Jared holds out his hand. He heads to the cage but halts me when I try to follow. "Amber, stay back."

What is it about these werewolves thinking they can give me orders? As soon as we're out of here, I'll remind them I'm the one who saved their fur-covered butts.

Another gunshot rings out, and I flinch.

Okay, maybe the saving is a team effort.

"Hurry," I say. Jared approaches the cage, hands up as if showing he has no weapons. With slow, careful movements, he starts to pick the lock. The stranger heads to the back of the cage. I notice both guys keep their eyes averted from each other.

Let the record reflect: *Wolves are into power games.* Because that's definitely what's going on here. Even little ole human me can sense it.

A rumbling sound comes from the hall, just as Jared gets the lock free on the strange wolf's cage. He springs back when the cage gate swings open.

I turn to figure out what's making the sound in the hall. In stalks Garrett's wolf, looking ten times bigger, eyes glowing like a demon's. It prowls forward, raising a nose to sniff the air, and then leaps over me, landing in front of Jared and the stranger. Wet spatters onto the ground. Something dark and liquid drips from the wolf's maw and side.

Blood.

Garrett's wolf roars. Jared cowers, and the Mexican wolf drops to his side to show his belly.

"No," I shout, and rush forward like a crazy woman. "Don't hurt them."

"Boss." Trey staggers in, naked, human form also covered in blood. "Easy, man."

Garrett's power rolls through the room, sending me to my knees. Jared and Trey drop to the floor. The stranger jumps back in the cage, in wolf form, and rolls on its back with a whine of submission. His eyes roll with terror.

"Garrett, come back to me." With effort, I raise my face. Whatever alpha weight he's throwing around, it affects me, but I can fight it. I stagger to my feet and approach the giant gray wolf, palms turned out. "Please. I need you."

Another roar, and Garrett starts to shift. He appears in human form, his head bowed, face twisted. When it's done, his chest heaves like he's done an Ironman. His muscles are slick with red, and his eyes still glow silver. I scan his torso to see if any of the blood is his and gasp when I see a bullet wound.

He gives a dismissive shake of his head. "It's nothing."

Jared and Trey rise slowly and put themselves between their alpha and the strange wolf in the cage who's still whimpering his submission. I notice they have matching wolf paw tattoos on their shoulders, like Garrett's. Must be a pack symbol.

"Garrett," I say, a bit breathless. He might be back in human form, but his predator self is still running the show. "What happened?" I ask at the same time Jared says, "The raiders—"

"Dead," Trey answers us both. "They're all dead."

Garrett wipes the blood from his mouth and flexes his fingers into fists.

I look away, to distract myself from what Garrett's done.

They were bad guys; they deserved it. It's still a lot for our second date.

"Did you find out anything about—?" Jared asks.

"No." With a roar, Garrett picks up a nearby cage and hurls it. "I lost control." Hearing the bitterness of self-censure, I step forward, longing to comfort him. But I don't know how.

He paces a few swift strides away, turns, and paces back, stabbing his fingers through his hair. "No one left to question now," he growls. His voice is barely human.

"What about him?" I tilt my head toward the strange wolf. He creeps forward and jumps lightly from the cage. Head lowered to the floor, he whines, as if waiting for permission.

"Shift," Garrett growls.

The strange wolf contorts and changes into human form. I keep my eyes above his waist. Ribs show through his brown skin, and his eyes are hollowed out with dark circles. Long hair falls around his eyes. I wonder how long he's been held prisoner.

Garrett prowls a circle around him. I step forward, between them, and he growls, picking me up with an arm around my waist, spinning, and setting me down behind him. Trey and Jared close in at his sides, making a human wall of protection, me behind it.

I clear my throat. "Do any of you speak Spanish?"

"You can translate from back there," Garrett rumbles.

I roll my eyes. "Señor, did you see a white wolf? Small female?" I ask in Spanish, raising my voice to get through the wall of wolf-men.

"*La Americana? Si.*" he answers.

I scuttle around to Jared's side to see the man, but Jared throws an arm out, keeping me back.

"Don't. Touch. Her," Garrett growls.

Jared drops his arm. "Not touching, Alpha."

"Where is she? Do you know where they took her?" I ask in Spanish.

"They sold her to the Montelobos. In the jungle."

I translate his answer. "Where in the jungle?" I ask sharply. "Do you know?"

"Monte Lobo."

Oh. Well, of course the Montelobos live in Monte Lobo. That's almost too easy. I pull my purse off my shoulder and thrust Garrett's phone at Trey. "Monte Lobo—in the jungle. Get Kylie on it."

After a glance at his alpha, the wolf grabs my phone and takes off. Jared goes with him.

"Is there anything else you can tell us?" I ask the stranger in Spanish, and repeat in English for Garrett's benefit.

He shakes his head. "Ask him how big their pack is, how strong."

I translate the question to the stranger.

"More than one hundred wolves," he says. "Well defended."

"Gracias, señor."

"A ustedes." He gives a half bow, backing away.

Jared walks in, dressed in cargo pants he must've found. He tosses clothes to Garrett and the strange wolf, who wrinkle their noses but dress quickly. "I found keys to their van outside. Trey's still trying to get through to Kylie, but we should get out of here."

"Will you be safe if we leave you?" I ask the strange wolf in Spanish.

He nods, explaining in rapid Spanish that he's from a small coastal town but has a strong pack there.

"All right. *Gracias*," I tell him, and we head out, down the hallway.

"Cover your eyes," Jared murmurs.

Before I understand what he means, a large warm hand closes over my eyes and an arm cinches around my waist. The way my senses leap up, I know it's Garrett. He's not gentle but steady and strong. My feet lift off the floor. I try not to think about the metallic smell of blood as Garrett carries me down the hall. Or what I'm not seeing.

Focus on Sedona.

Once we're outside, he drops me to the ground, and I take deep breaths.

Garrett spins me around and peers into my face with all-silver eyes. "Are you hurt? Tell me you're not fucking hurt, or I'll go back and kill those guys a second time."

The violence of his assertion ought to frighten me, but it doesn't. It's for me. All that passion is for me. "Not hurt," I whisper.

He yanks me against him, crushing my body to his so tightly I can't breathe.

"Easy, Alpha," I choke.

He releases me abruptly and paces away, as if afraid to be too near me.

Trey trots up to us, cell in hand. "I don't have a cell signal to get through to Kylie. Let's go to the hotel, and look it up ourselves."

Garrett nods, grim. "I need to call my dad for reinforcements. We're not going into Monte Lobo alone."

"I already did," I admit, wincing as six pairs of glowing eyes swing to me. "I wasn't sure I would make it out of the warehouse, and I didn't want to..." The low growling coming from Garrett's chest warns me I'm worrying his wolf again. "Your dad's on his way."

8

Garrett

I can't speak the entire ride to the hotel. I'm barely staying in human form. I've never been so on edge, so close to losing it. No—fuck that—I already lost it. I went savage on those guys back at the warehouse when the situation called for intelligence. If the guy in the cage hadn't given us a lead, we'd be no closer to finding Sedona right now, thanks to me.

The whole evening was a cluster-fuck. We showed up at the textile factory. Like most of the buildings in Mexico City, it was all concrete on the outside, no way to see in. I sent Jared and Trey in one direction around the building, and I went the other.

When we met up, some asshole had Trey in a headlock, a gun pointed at his head. "*Manos arriba*," the motherfucker yelled.

I didn't have to understand Spanish to know what he wanted. I had no choice but to put my hands in the air and climb into the fucking cages that lined the warehouse. A wolf can survive a gunshot wound, but not to the head.

Only shifter I know who survived a gunshot to the head is an elderly panther in Tucson, and she was extremely lucky the shots didn't hit anything vital. I wasn't about to risk Trey's life.

But the second I was in the cage, I shifted, shredding my clothes. The place reeked of wolves, but I swear I picked up Sedona's scent. I tried to bust through my cage with sheer force, but they weren't ordinary dog cages. No, these guys knew what they were doing. The cages were made of reinforced steel. If Amber hadn't shown up—

I growl in the backseat of the van, and Amber turns her lovely blue eyes up to me. I don't know why the fuck she's not afraid of me when I'm like this. She sure as hell should be.

My wolf is ready to break out and rip more throats just thinking about Amber being back there, putting herself in danger for us.

I want to turn her over my knee and smack her pretty ass red for it, but I know it's not safe for me to touch her. Not that I'd hurt her—not that way, anyway. But I'm inches away from marking her. Between the full moon and my wolf's desire to protect her by forever imprinting her with my scent, I'm shaking from the effort of keeping it together with her.

We get to the hotel and I head straight for the shower. Maybe if I rid myself of the scent of blood, I'll be able to calm the fuck down. Doubtful. But it's worth a shot.

I strip out of the too-small pants and step into the spray of water, pinching my wound to expel the bullet my body has already sent to the surface.

I remember the way my little lawyer paled when she saw

the wound, the horror that streaked her face. Damn, I've done nothing to earn that concern, but I sure as hell am going to try to be worthy from here on out. And I *have* to do a better job keeping her safe. Fates, she could've been taken prisoner, too, and we'd all be locked up now. Or worse.

I ought to be grateful to her, but instead I'm just pissed. Pissed she had to put herself at risk to rescue me. A growl reverberates in my throat.

I turn the water to cold. It does nothing to cool my burning skin, to stomp down the wolf.

Mark her mark her mark her.

I'm burning to sink my teeth into Amber's ripe flesh. Make her forever mine. I'm burning to sink my cock into her sweet little body, feel what it's like to move inside her. I bet she's tight as fuck. Like heaven. Maybe there's some way I could fuck her without marking her.

I can't tell if it's my wolf or my own mind trying to talk me into doing what can't be done, but I want her with a desperation that makes my canines pop out, dripping with the serum to mark her. I bite my own lip and draw blood.

My tough-as-nails little lawyer is all gooey soft inside. A giant heart made of soft downy feathers. I'd give anything to earn the right to call her mine. What would it be like to have Amber beneath me? I'm dying to see her look up at me with those big blue eyes, trust shining bright, her small body yielding and sweet. *Fuuuuuuck.*

I turn off the water and wrap a towel around my waist. My wound has already stopped bleeding, the edges starting to close.

We booked a suite, with two beds in one room and a living area in the other. Trey and Jared are in the living room, and I want to howl because Amber's with them. Which is all kinds of stupid, because while I know they'd die for her, it's only because they know she's mine. And my guys are rock solid. They would never, ever fuck with what's mine.

Still, I slam my fist down on the dresser. I want to tear the room apart.

I don't know how I'm going to survive the night in the same hotel suite as Amber.

~.~

Amber

It sounds like Garrett is throwing things in the bedroom. I sense his agitation through the wall. Guilt, anger, frustration roll off him in waves. Have I always known exactly how people feel? Or is it just him?

Trey looks in the direction of the bedroom then shoots a concerned glance at Jared. We're sitting around the small table. They finished my *torta* in about three seconds flat and have ordered more food from room service. "I've never seen him this close to losing control," Trey mutters.

"I know."

"What's wrong with him?" I ask.

Jared fiddles with a book of matches that were on the coffee table, spinning it on its edge. "Full moon. Sister's missing. And you."

"What about me?"

"He was scared for you back there. I think he's still pissed off. He's really got it bad for you, Amber." The matchbook spins to a stop. He picks it up and starts it again.

My heart leaps then trips and falls. "But wolves can't be with humans."

"That's a problem. But it doesn't matter to his wolf. The animal's claimed you. Once our wolf makes its choice, that's it. You have to mate or—"

"Or?"

"Or your animal might go moon mad," Trey supplies, fiddling his lip piercing with his tongue.

"What is moon mad?" I ask.

"They turn animal and can't change back. They're lost forever. It doesn't happen with every wolf," Trey explains.

"Only the most dominant ones," Jared says.

I swallow hard. Garrett is as dominant as they come. But he doesn't want to mate me. He already told me it can't work. "Do wolves ever mate with humans?"

"Sometimes," Jared says with a shrug. "But mating with humans is discouraged by most packs. And an alpha male takes an alpha female."

I hear the subtext. *Not a wimpy human.*

"Garrett's dad wouldn't like it." Trey snatches the book of matches from Jared's fingers and taps it open, pulling one out.

Great. I've already made a bad impression.

"But there are many who believe there's only one true mate for each wolf. And the wolf recognizes his mate when he sees her. Being near her both riles him up and calms him down." He strikes a match against the side of the box and flicks the burning stick at Jared, who yelps and dodges it with a grin. "That's what he's like with you."

Amber Drake, psychic. Tamer of werewolves. Maybe I'll hang that shingle after all.

A thud sounds from the bedroom, like Garrett put his fist through the wall. *Good thing the room's not on my credit card.* If he's upset over me, it's my job to defuse it. I push open the door and step inside, closing it behind me. I ought to be afraid, but I'm not. "Hey. Are you mad at me?"

"No," he snarls, whirling. I sense his pain.

"You're upset because I was in danger? Why don't you talk to me about it?"

He stalks over, eyes flashing silver. Picking me up by waist, he pins me against the wall, holding me at nose level. "Baby, you scared the fuck out of me. You could've been captured. Or hurt. Or killed," he growls. "Do you think I could live with myself if anything ever happened to you?"

I can't speak. A lump forms in my throat. Has anyone ever cared so much about what happens to me?

"Well, I couldn't. I wouldn't be able to go on."

"Garrett." The extent of his anguish stuns me, cracking some hardened piece of armor that's been around my heart for most of my life. Someone cares—about me.

"I ought to turn your cute little ass red." He drops me to the floor and cradles my cheek. His touch is far gentler than I expected. He leans his forehead against mine. "You do *not* put your own safety at risk for me. I am a shifter—I heal almost instantly. You are *human*."

Yeah, I got that, big guy.

"You could've been shot or had your throat torn out tonight," he goes on. "What if they took you for breeding?"

"But I'm not a wolf."

"Don't argue with me." He pulls me into a rough embrace, his huge arms wrapping around my waist. He drags his lips up the column of my neck. "You're *mine*, dammit. I can't let anything happen to you. Do you understand?"

"I understand," I whisper as the words *you're mine* knock around in my head, causing my brain to short circuit. For someone who never belonged, nothing could sound sweeter. And, somehow, I do belong with Garrett. Even though I am human and he is wolf. Even though we have nothing in common—I am his and he is mine. A simple equation with no basis in logic. Only in love.

Except he told me last night he can't be with me.

He palms my ass and squeezes. "I reserve the right to punish this juicy ass later." His voice is deep and gravelly.

I give a husky laugh. "Sorry, there's no retrial."

He tongues my earlobe. "I'll have to do it now, then." He turns me to face away from him. "Hands on the wall." The deep command sounds like pure seduction. He slides his palms slowly down my arms to grip my wrists and lift them to the cool plaster. "Don't move them. If you do, I'll double your punishment."

I waggle my ass, only excited by his threat. This man—wolf—wants me. Needs me, even. I've never felt so desirable in my life.

His fingers work the button on my jeans open, and he hooks his thumbs in the waistband of both the jeans and my panties and drags them over my hips. They drop in a puddle at my feet.

"What's my sentence?" I say hoarsely, stepping out of them.

He lands a hard slap on my ass. "This." He strokes both palms over my bare ass and squeezes. Slaps again. "I want you," he says gruffly, unpinning my hair from its French twist. It falls over one shoulder. He slips his fingers under my T-shirt and glides them up until they reach my breasts. With a flick, he opens the front closure on my bra and cups my swelling girls.

"You're so fucking beautiful, Amber. I've wanted you since the moment you cocked that hip and gave me attitude in the elevator. I don't know how I've kept from fucking you senseless." His voice is thick.

"What are you waiting for?" I dare.

His sharp intake of breath has me biting my lip. One quick movement and my shirt and bra fly over my head. "Hands back up." He pins my wrists against the wall with one palm, smacks my ass with the other.

My pussy clenches, excitement coursing through me. "I'm on the pill," I whisper.

An inhuman growl fills the room. "Why?" he roars.

I try to turn, but he keeps his hand closed over my wrists. "For heavy periods. Jeez, Garrett."

I feel him sag behind me. "Thank fuck. Don't ever tell me about another man unless you want me to rip his throat out."

"Too much, Garrett." My voice is shaky, but some part of me is thrilled with his possessiveness. His jealousy. I want him to fully claim me the way no one has.

He runs his hands up the length of my bare back, wraps them around the front to pinch my nipples between his fingers. "I need you, baby." His teeth graze my shoulder. "I need you so fucking badly."

I try to pry my fingers from the wall again, planning to turn and help him get on with things, but clearly, he's the one in control. He slaps a hand over mine, pinning them back in place. A low growl of disapproval rumbles beside my ear.

His free hand slides down my fluttering belly to cup my mons.

I'm already soaked for him, my legs shaking.

He sweeps the pad of one large finger over my slit, gliding in my juices. "Tell me about this pussy, Counselor," he rumbles in a low voice. "Has she missed me?"

"Y-yes."

"Tell me I'm the only one who gets her wet." He taps my clit.

"You're the one," I murmur. "I mean, the only one."

"I'd love to taste her again, but I'm having a hard time dialing it back. I promise I'll give her the best licking of her life when the moon isn't so goddamn full."

I realize his breath is sawing in and out like he's running a race. Like it's taking all his effort not to attack.

I don't want him to hold back. With a desperation that might very well match his, I want him, to get on with it

"Take me, Garrett." I push my ass out, hoping to tempt him.

"Fuck." I hear the rustle of his jeans hitting the floor. "I'm not sure I can do this, baby. I don't want to hurt you."

"You won't," I promise. I never thought I'd be the type to like rough sex, but at this moment, I'd give anything for a nice, hard fuck. Lawyer Amber is appalled.

Garrett growls and rubs the head of his cock over my entrance, slicking it in my juices.

"Yes," I breathe. "Take me."

His breath rasps in my ear. He holds my waist and presses in, filling me, stretching me wide with his enormous cock.

My pussy clenches around him, and I gasp at the intensity. My eyeballs roll back in my head. "Don't stop, I need you in me."

His breath stops altogether then comes hot on my ear as he eases in, filling me. He crushes my breast in his hand and begins to pump in and out, his hips slapping against my ass.

My head grows light. The pleasure is like none I've experienced. Wolf cock, indeed. Yeah, it's definitely better. He pummels me, the head of his cock hitting my inner wall. It's incredible. Miraculous, even.

I realize I've never, in my twenty-six years, been properly fucked. Never been taken from behind, even. Never done it standing up. Never had sex with my lover's hot handprints burning my ass cheeks.

Yeah. Garrett has been a flurry of firsts for me and this one is coming close to blowing my ever-loving mind. And somehow I have a feeling there's so much more. This is just the tip of the iceberg when it comes to sex with Garrett.

His fingers tighten on my hip. "Oh God," he mutters, and pounds harder.

"Fuck, Amber—I can't—" An inhuman growl cuts off his speech, and he pulls out. I gasp and look over my shoulder to see him stumble back, his eyes glowing silver, fangs bared.

Fangs? He's still in human form. Why in the hell does he have fangs?

He shakes his head like a dog shakes off water. "Amber." His voice is so guttural, I barely understand him. "Get your clothes on and get out."

"What? No."

The cords in his neck pop out. His muscles ripple and strain. "*Now,* Amber." The hurt must show on my face, because he looks stricken. "I'm sorry," he mutters. "I'm sorry, Amber. But I need you to get out. For your own good. *Please.* Get out." He stalks to the bathroom and shuts himself in.

Reeling, I pick up my clothing and put it on with shaking hands. Let the record reflect: *I have no fucking clue what just happened.*

I don't want to leave, but I have to honor Garrett's request, so I open the bedroom door and walk out.

Trey is still at the table, eating the food that's been delivered. He glances at me then does a double take. "Are you all right?"

Dammit. Tears streak freely down my cheeks.

He stands and opens his arms. "Come here."

I stumble forward, leaning into his lanky frame as he wraps me in a hug.

"Are you okay?" he repeats.

I don't mean to tell him anything. But I hadn't meant to let them see me cry, either. "His teeth got long, and his eyes changed color," I blurt on a sob. "He told me to get out."

Trey shares a glance with Jared across the room.

"Damn," Jared mutters.

"What?"

Trey blows his breath out. "He wants to mark you, Amber. Do you know what that means?"

I shake my head. No idea.

"It's the way wolves mate—the male sinks his teeth into the female to permanently leave his scent. We're quite territorial with our females. Once you're marked, you're mated for life. But he can't mark you, because you're human. At best, it can cause terrible scarring. At worst, it could kill you. He can't control himself right now, so he's trying to protect you."

A vision flickers before my eyes: *I'm standing in front of a mirror, lifting my hair away from my shoulder to examine a scar.*

The bedroom door opens with a bang, and Garrett looms in the doorway, brows tight around his silver eyes.

Trey shoves me away from his body and holds up his hands. "Not touching h—"

A flash of movement and a snarl and Garrett flies through the air and knocks Trey to the floor.

"A little help," Trey gasps as he rolls away, not fighting back but moving quickly to extricate himself.

Garrett pins Trey down with his forearm across the wolf's windpipe.

"Garrett, stop!" I scream.

He turns his glittering gaze on me and lunges, grasping my waist and pulling me down on top of him. His hands burn like brands; heat suffusing my skin everywhere he touches. He yanks my shirt up as if he intends to pull it off me, his fangs bared and gleaming.

Clearly, he's more beast than man, now, and considering how cautious his friends are, I admit I'm scared.

I scream. Jared seizes me from behind, pulling me back off Garrett.

He roars his displeasure and leaps to his feet after me. Trey catches him from behind before he reaches me, and Jared puts his body in front of mine, joining Trey in the fight against Garrett. The two younger wolves push Garrett backward, pinning him to a wall, leaning their full weight against him to hold him there.

"Go into the bedroom and lock the door, hon," Trey says.

Garrett roars again, pulling free of the wall, only to be slammed back by the two younger wolves.

"Sorry! I didn't mean to call her *hon*. *Amber*, get in the bedroom. Now," Trey barks.

But I can't let this go on. Garrett is suffering because of his need for me, and his friends are risking their lives to protect me from him. I ignore the directive, and walk, instead, to Garrett. I lay my palm flat on his bulging chest. "I'm not afraid of him." I keep my eyes glued to Garrett's silver ones.

I swear I see the spark of recognition, the flicker of blue in his silver eyes.

"You'd better be," Jared grits, obviously struggling with all his might to hold Garrett back.

I ignore Trey and Jared and catch Garrett's gaze, holding it. *"Mark me."*

He lunges forward again, but when the boys throw him back against the wall, he gives his head a shake. "I'll tear you apart, Counselor. Get. Out of here. Please."

"No. I've seen how this one ends. I want you to mark me."

Garrett stills, his breath rasping in his chest. "What?"

I nod. "You need to mark me." I turn to the younger wolves. "Let him go."

They look to Garrett, who stares at me a long time before nodding. The boys ease their weight back from his shoulders, appearing ready to tackle him again at a moment's notice.

He picks me up, and I straddle his waist, looping my arms around his thick neck. He looks up into my face. "Are you sure?"

I nod. Even though my heart thunders, I trust him. He would never hurt me if he could help it.

9

Garrett

E ven with the wolf screaming to be set free, my mind works to be present for Amber. "Baby, do you understand what this means?" I ask as I carry her to the bedroom. I don't know how she even knows about marking.

"Yes," she whispers. "That you'll mate me for life."

"That's right. Once I've marked you, I'll never let you go —not for any reason. I'd follow you to the ends of the Earth to keep what's mine."

Miraculously, she doesn't seem disturbed by that. My tough little independent lawyer appears to be willingly giving herself over to me.

"Do you hear me? You will belong to me. Forever. You'll be mine to protect and hold. To pleasure."

"I want you to mark me," she repeats, seemingly undaunted by my words.

I shut the door behind us. "Do you know what it involves? I'll have to bite you, Amber. A wolf bite. It will definitely hurt, and most likely scar you." *And if I fuck up, I could kill you.* Fates, I don't want to do this to her. She doesn't deserve this kind of trauma.

She nods. "I saw the scars—in a vision. That's how I know this needs to happen."

A vision. Thank the fates. I can't be making a mistake if she saw it.

I sit down on a chair, Amber straddling my lap. I figure I need to stay on the bottom. Anything to slow me down, keep me from mauling her. I palm her ass cheeks in both my hands, squeeze them. She rocks her pelvis down, grinding over my rock-hard cock.

I tug her shirt off and unhook the pale-pink bra. It's sweet and delicate, like her. She definitely doesn't belong with a guy like me, but I can't stop myself from claiming her, now that she's offered.

My position in the pack will be altered. My dad's predictions that I'd never be able to lead my own pack will prove true. I don't give a fuck. Amber's mine. I need her, like a wolf needs to run.

Her perky breasts spring out of their satin enclosure, and I attack one, sucking the stiff bud into my mouth.

Amber lets out a wanton cry that nearly has me jizzing in my jeans. I'm one stroke away from coming, as it is. One breath away from piercing her with my lengthening teeth. The second I sink into her, I'm going to go off like a cannon. But I owe her so much more than that. I don't want her to remember her marking as only pain and trauma.

I turn my attention to her other nipple, flicking it with my tongue, grazing my teeth over it.

"Shirt off," she murmurs.

"Hmm?"

She hooks a finger in the collar of my T-shirt. "I want your shirt off, too."

I smile through my haze of lust, drunk on desire, and peel off my T-shirt. She runs her hands over my pecs and arches into me, rubbing those beautiful tits against my bare skin.

A growl erupts from my throat. I have to mark her soon.

"I need to be inside you, baby." I lick a line from her solar plexus to her throat.

She wriggles off me and loses the rest of her clothing. "Good," she encourages.

"No," I groan. My breath comes in short little pants now as it takes all my effort not to throw her to the floor and pound into her until she splits in two. "I doubt it will be any good. I'm going to come the second I'm inside you." I unbutton my jeans and release my straining cock.

I pull her onto my lap, facing away, and bring my fingers to the notch between her thighs. "I'll make it up to you later, I promise," I manage to say. "I'll make it up for the rest of our goddamn lives."

A shiver runs through Amber. I don't know what it means. I sure as hell hope it wasn't foreboding.

But her pussy is wet. I know she wants me. I rub the head of my cock along her dewy slit. My entire body shakes with the effort it takes to keep myself in check. Every cell in my body screams for me to throw her down and fuck her roughly, marking her forever with my teeth.

She shifts to line her sweet channel up with my throbbing length, and I snap my hips, spearing into her. A shudder of satisfaction runs through my body. Like I've just found home.

Nothing has ever felt so right in my life. My vision domes and sharpens as the animal in me surges forward. I grasp Amber's waist and lift and lower her over my cock, hoping to the fates I'm not bruising her, not scaring her with how hard I grip, how deep I thrust.

My hips lift to meet hers and I'm falling, falling into deeper, darker need.

She's making encouraging sounds—wanton sounds.

"Amber... Amber... I want... I need—" Fates I can't even put together a sentence. I bounce her over my rigid cock like I'll die if I don't get enough. If I don't get deeper. Faster.

I squeeze my eyes shut, fighting back the impulse to fully claim her. I pull her over my cock hard and fast, owning her body, dominating it completely as I wrestle with my wolf for control.

"Yes, Garrett," she cries out.

"Who do you belong to?" I snarl, riding a wave of lust so high I'm delirious. Each thrust into her tight channel makes me crazier.

"You! Please, Garrett, I'm so close."

"I'll give you what you need," I growl, hoping I can deliver because the fever that's taken over me is hotter than magma. I stand and bend her at the waist like a rag doll. Now I can drill into her with more force.

She screams. "There! Oh God, right there. Oh God, don't stop, don't stop, pleeeeeease." She tumbles over the crest into orgasm. The moment her tight little pussy clamps down on my cock, the leash on the wolf snaps.

My movements grow jerky as she continues to squeeze my cock with her finish. Growls fill the room and I open my eyes, realize I'm making the sound. My fangs drip with the secretion to embed into her flesh. I want to give it to her so badly. Every muscle is coiled, ready to spring.

And just like that, I go off. Cum shoots up my shaft. I sit and yank her down tight in my lap, my feet stomping on the floor, a roar echoing off the walls. If she were a wolf, I'd bite the back of her neck, but I have to be so fucking careful. I sweep her pale blonde hair from her neck and sink my teeth down on the fleshy part of her trapezius, where I'm least likely to seriously injure her.

I hold back the torrent of energy demanding I snap my jaws with force, bury those teeth deeper into her flesh.

She cries out, and I squeeze my eyes closed against the surge of guilt. My stupid cock doesn't get the message, and I come again, thrusting into her. Shaking, I extricate my fangs from her flesh and lick the wound clean. The antibodies in my saliva should speed her recovery. "It's over, baby. I'm so sorry." I grab my T-shirt and ball it up to press against the wounds and staunch any flow of blood.

Amber gives another gasp and a whimper. She turns to look at me, and her wide blue eyes fill with tears.

"Oh fates," I choke, my own eyes smarting.

She touches my face. "No, it's okay, it's okay, it's okay."

I lift her from my lap and grab the blanket from the bed, wrapping it around her.

I must look horrified, because she holds up her hand. "I'm okay. I'm okay." But—*fuck!*—blood's soaking through the shirt at her shoulder. I want to smash things, everything within reach. My female is hurt, and it's my fault.

"Amber." I speak her name like a prayer. Like a lament. A beg for forgiveness, even though she's already granted it.

A knock sounds at the door. "Everything okay?" Trey asks through the wood.

I lift Amber and ease her onto the bed then pull on my jeans and open the door. Trey stands there, Jared behind him.

I've never been more grateful for my pack mates' support, especially considering I just tried to smash their faces in. "Do you think she needs stitches? Or whatever it is humans do for wounds?"

Trey walks in, radiating calm. "Let me see it." He takes the shirt from Amber and peers at the wounds. "No. these look okay to me. No major arteries. I think she'll be okay. They don't do stitches for puncture wounds anyway; they want them to get air to prevent infection."

Thank fuck. I hope to hell he knows what he's talking about.

Jared produces a bottle of Spanish-labeled pain reducers. "I went out to get you some ibuprofen," he says to Amber. "And coconut oil because it's supposed to be anti-bacterial and anti-fungal."

"Not for a major wound, you idiot," Trey says and Jared punches him.

"And I have liquor, too, if you prefer that." Jared holds out a bottle of Jose Cuervo.

I shove the bottle of Cuervo away. "No liquor. Yes on the painkillers. Can you get her a glass of water?"

Amber accepts the ibuprofen. She's looking pale, which fucking kills me, so I scoop her up and climb to the head of the bed, settling with her cradled against my chest.

Jared returns with the glass of water and three ibuprofen. "Do you need anything else?"

I shake my head.

"All right, we'll leave you alone, then."

The two boys walk out. Maybe it's because my chest has been ripped up, leaving my heart standing open and unprotected, but my gratitude for their loyalty overwhelms me.

~.~

Amber

I lean back against Garrett's solid chest. "I feel...kinda weird."

"The serum that coated my teeth contains a drug that will make you a little high. It calms the female after she's been mauled."

"Is this dangerous for female wolves, too?"

He shook his head. "No. shifters have incredible healing capacities. It would be a temporary pain for a she-wolf. She'd be out of pain in a few hours, healed by morning." He strokes my hair back from my face, worry etched in the lines of his face.

"I'll be fine, too."

He runs his thumb along my cheek. "You are incredibly brave. You're alpha material, even if you aren't a wolf."

I study him. "What does that mean, exactly?"

His face closes, as if he has something to hide. "Nothing. Just that you're a good mate for an alpha."

Ah. I understand now. "Except that an alpha's mate should be a wolf."

His jaw tightens. "I don't care about that."

I don't have to be psychic to know he's hiding something. Protecting me from something. *Shitballs.* My certainty about wanting to be marked erodes. "So it's a problem that I'm human? Of course it is," I answer my own question. "Because you won't produce shifter offspring."

"May not," he corrects. "And that's inconsequential. Me being alpha is of no matter, either," he declares.

Goose bumps stand up on my skin. My head's foggy from the drug in the serum, and I give it a shake to clear it. "Wait...you might lose your position as alpha? Because you're mated to me?"

His face hardens. "You're not just a human. You're a para-normal, with second sight. You're a perfect mate for an alpha," he repeats as if speaking directly to my would-be detractors.

My vision blurs. "I'm sorry."

"No," he says fiercely. "Not sorry. You'd better not be sorry for me, because I'm the lucky son-of-a-bitch who found his fated mate. Do you think the urge to mark happens every full moon, with any female? It doesn't. I've never felt it before I met you. So, I may have held back, but it wasn't because I was worried about losing my position as alpha or of the stigma of mating with a human, or anything like that. Do you understand me?" He cups my chin. "It was only out of my fear of hurting you, and because it wasn't fair to claim you under these circumstances."

"What circumstances?"

His face clouds. "I strong-armed you into helping me. I brought you here against your will. You hardly know me. And you have no idea what you've gotten yourself into by mating with me."

The serum has relaxed me now, taking away the agitation and sharpness of the pain. "What have I gotten myself into?" I bring a teasing lilt to my voice. "A dominant wolf who threatens to spank me when I don't follow orders?" Just saying the words reactivates my lust from earlier, and when Garrett inhales sharply, I know he's scented my arousal.

"You have a mate who's going to use your little body any and every way he pleases, anytime, anywhere," he growls in my ear. Wrapping a fist in my hair, he tugs my head back.

My pussy clenches.

"When you displease me, I will pull down your panties and spank you with my hand. I'll shove my big cock in your ass, and I won't let you come."

A shocked giggle comes out of my mouth. My body turns to liquid desire as orgasm looms close without my lady bits even being touched. He seems to know because he slides his thick fingers between my thighs, finding the swollen nub of my clit.

"I'll tie you to the bed and fuck you senseless. And when I'm finished, I'll shove a big plug in your ass and spank you, just because I feel like it."

"Y-you're crazy," I mutter, but my thighs scissor together, and an orgasm rips through me. My pelvic-floor muscles lift as my pussy contracts in a series of waves.

Garrett palms my nape. "Damn, girl, even having marked you, I don't know how to make it through the night without fucking you six ways until Sunday."

"What's holding you back?" I ask in my best bedroom voice.

"The open wounds on your shoulder." That killed the mood. "And knowing my father will be here soon."

A flash of knowing flickers. "He's here now," I say, just before a loud knock sounds on the suite door.

10

Garrett

"Y ou wait here, baby." I ease her from my lap onto the bed. I doubt my dad will greet our mating with celebration, and I'll be damned if I'm going to subject Amber to his reaction.

She looks adorable, hair tousled and eyes bright with that freshly fucked sort of look. Her color has come back, thank the fates. I stamp my mouth over her full lips and back away, hardly able to tear my eyes from her. *My human. My mate.* I can hardly believe it.

Jared already let my father and the top three of his pack in, and they crowd the hotel suite wearing grim expressions. A fresh stab of shame over my inability to retrieve Sedona shoots through me as I step forward to shake my father's hand. He's not the hugging sort of father—he maintains his cold authority from a distance, even over his family members.

"Son." He clasps my hand. "What in the hell is going on?"

"Sedona was kidnapped by wolves while on a spring break trip to San Carlos. She's in a remote area called Monte Lobo. With your reinforcements, we plan to go break her out at first light."

"You should have called me right away."

I expected this critique, but it still makes my chest heavy. "I know. I wanted to take care of it without worrying you, but you're right, and I'm sorry."

My father gazes at me, his steely gray eyes hard, the lines on his face making him look so much older than I remembered. I realize, with a start, he would no longer win in a contest between us for alpha, not that I'd ever challenge him. My dad nods, once. "Who the hell is Amber?"

As if on cue, my little human toddles from the bedroom, dressed but looking slightly woozy. My heart lurches. I hold my arm out, and she ducks under it, nestles against my side.

"Amber Drake, sir." She extends her hand. I don't know how she knows to call him *sir*, but I appreciate her ability to adapt to the situation. She's just a slip of a thing, but I see her grow taller, her back straighten. She must be a formidable enemy in the courtroom.

"She's my mate." I lace my words with a touch of steel to warn my father against any insults. He may not approve, but it's done, and he'll have to get used to it.

My father's gaze travels to the fresh wound on her shoulder then rest on her face. He gives her a stern look, as if she's one of his pack members. "I told you to stay put, young lady."

"Lay off," I growl, but Amber seems unfazed.

"I know, sir."

My father continues to glower at Amber, who, amazingly, doesn't cower. If she showed the slightest sign of distress, I would've taken my father on right then and there —prove who's the alpha now.

"So you went to rescue these wolves all by yourself?"

Amber lifts her chin the way she did the night I met her in the elevator, refusing to show intimidation. "I had to, sir. I was shown it in a vision."

"You didn't mention that to me." It eases some of my guilt and angst over her being at risk.

"You weren't in a chatty mood." She glances up at me from under her lashes, making my heart jump and bang against my ribs. Such a small thing, and she has me wrapped around her finger so tightly.

"So you're shown things?" my father asks. Skepticism scrawls across his features.

Amber nods. "Sometimes, sir. I can't always control it." Her face contorts in a grimace of pain.

Fates, it's the bite wounds. I pull her closer to my side, ready to rush her to the hospital at the drop of a hat.

"Sedona's been mated," Amber chokes out.

Her wince was a vision, not the marking.

"But her mate didn't kidnap her. He's working to get her free."

"Her *mate*?" my father snaps.

Amber's eyes fly wide, as if her revelation surprises even her. She looks past my father, her focus going soft. "Yes...they were locked together over the full moon. He marked her."

"You know where she is?" my dad snaps, looking at me.

I nod.

"Then let's move. We have three vans of wolves waiting on the street. No humans."

Even though I agree, I hate the way he gives the order without even looking at Amber.

I turn to her and cup her cheek. "I need you to stay here, baby. I won't need it, but this time don't even think about rescuing me. No matter what your visions show you. Understand?"

She nods. There's a trace of sadness to her that I can't pinpoint, but my dad is already pushing everyone out the door.

"Trey, you stay with Amber. In case her wounds turn bad," I order.

"No, I'm fine," she interjects. "Totally fine. You guys go."

I hesitate, torn between wanting to be fully prepared when we get Sedona and my concern over Amber.

She pushes us out the door. "I'm fine. I'll lock the door, order room service, and wait for you to come back."

"Okay," I relent. I bend to kiss her. "Get some rest, baby. Sleep in tomorrow. I'll call you on the hotel phone with an update."

She lifts her lips and kisses me back, and I reluctantly leave her. Her face is shadowed, and the only way I can convince my wolf to leave her is vowing silently to return.

~.~

Amber

Nausea hits me the minute they leave. Between the drugged out feeling from being marked, the pain and general exhaustion, my body rebels at what I know I need to do—

Leave.

If I'd known Garrett would lose his position as alpha by marking me, I never would have let him do it. His pack is everything to him. I've seen how tight they are—closer than family. They care for each other, have each other's backs. His guys would do anything for him. He has a pack tattoo on his arm, for God's sake.

Loneliness shoots through me, just contemplating leaving him. Before I met Garrett, I managed my loneliness. Used measures of order, control, and a sense of contributing to society to keep my life on the upswing.

But now I see all those things for what they were—a mask to hide the truth that's always gnawed at me. I'm alone in the world.

Which is fine. Not everyone can be from big packs or families. I've learned to manage on my own, and I'll manage without Garrett, too. I have my job. And my best friend. And foster kids who need my help. Well, yeah, that's my job.

We were only mated for a few hours. I've only considered him my boyfriend for a day.

Letting go won't be that hard.

Yeah, right.

My eyes burn as I throw my things into the silver rolling suitcase I filled when Garrett ordered me to pack. Every time I waver into self-pity, I remind myself I'm doing this for Garrett. He deserves an alpha wolf for a mate.

Not Crazy Amber.

Definitely not Crazy Amber.

I don't want Crazy Amber—how could she be what Garrett wants?

No, his worry over Sedona, the full moon, and their proximity made him impetuous. Sooner or later, he'd realize he made a mistake. Maybe next week. Maybe in a month. Maybe not for three months. But it would happen, like the inevitability of the next moonrise. Better to rip the Band-Aid off quickly. Or leave before more damage is done. Or whichever saying best fits.

It's been a wild weekend, but that's all it was. Wild. And a weekend.

I leave the hotel room and take the elevator down to the lobby. It's past midnight, but I find a cab outside and ask to go to the airport.

As I ride away, my head begins to throb. I pull the bottle of ibuprofen Trey brought me out of my purse and pop three, even though I know they won't do any good. I stare at the dark streets whizzing by and brace myself against the pain. Not in my head but from the giant javelin lanced through my chest.

I'll get by. I always do.

In the airport, I check the departures and find one going to Phoenix at six a.m. It's two hours from Tucson but close enough. I pay for a ticket and sit down in a chair to wait for morning.

The visions come the moment I close my eyes. I fight them back, but it feels like my head will explode. I see fast-forward movies playing of Sedona, a beautiful brunette, locked in a sparsely-furnished room with a young Mexican man. It blurs and shifts into a fight between the young man and the wolves who guard the door. Then, the two of them, standing on a beautiful veranda that overlooks a vast jungle. The van Trey stole from the warehouse drives in on the road below.

Garrett.

My body grieves for him, as if he didn't embed just his scent, but his very essence in me, making me forever addicted to him. I shove the visions back, swallow them down. My legs are shaky when I stand, but I walk to the bathroom to splash cold water on my face. It's almost morning. My plane will leave soon, and I can sleep on it.

Tomorrow, I'll be home, and I can go about pretending this never happened.

I look in the mirror, but I don't see myself, I see the white-haired woman from the airport restroom years before. She stares back at me with accusation in her eyes.

"I'm sorry," I choke, but the room is spinning. It's all I can do to hang onto the counter and not fall down.

The last thing I remember is my vision going black right before my head strikes something hard and I blessedly lose consciousness.

~.~

Garrett

I sit in the passenger side of a twenty-passenger van and crack my tattooed knuckles. We have three giant vans—more like mini buses—driving in a caravan into the jungle. My father brought sixty men with him. The Montelobos have over one hundred. Decent odds, considering how ferocious my home pack can be. Still, it's the first time I've gone into a fight with someone waiting for me to return.

Life feels more precious now. My own life, Amber's. Certainly Sedona's. Fates, she's just a kid, still. This shouldn't have happened to her.

I ride in the van with my pack members, to let them know how much I appreciate their support. How important this battle is to me. I'm not going to go in there and lose. Losing isn't in my blood, especially not where Sedona's involved. Since the same blood runs through my father's veins, I know we're undefeatable.

The drive takes two and a half hours. Enough time for

me to replay every moment I've spent with Amber, from the day I met her until the minute I left her at the hotel. In a short amount of time, she's completely changed my life.

I feel so far removed from the never-willing-to-settle-down party boy I was a week ago. The guy my dad rode hard for not manning up and acting like a true leader. The guy who didn't take much seriously. Yes, I was a successful businessman, but it hadn't been hard. I had the Midas touch. I got in the real estate market at the right time. My dad provided me with initial start-up capital, but I was able to pay him back within a year. The rest I did on my own.

It's so easy to see now that I played the rebel out of fear of becoming my dad. Fear of becoming an uptight asshole who rides his pack and family hard.

Except now that my own instincts to protect those precious to me—Amber and Sedona, and my pack members, too—have kicked into high gear, I understand where he was coming from. I've made different choices in my leadership style, but we probably both want the same things. And now that I have a mate, it's obvious to me I need to grow up.

I need to be the kind of man Amber would be proud to introduce to her colleagues. Her foster kids. That doesn't mean I'm going to put on a suit and tie, but it's time to stop living like a frat boy.

The van winds up a narrow dirt road, climbing higher and higher into dense rainforest. Everything looks rural and poor until we stop by a high-tech electric security gate. My dad and I get out. I smash the security camera staring down at us and help him rip the gate from its hinges, bending and tearing the metal.

I'm ready to shift right there and run in on four paws, but my dad orders the vans to drive in farther. I tear my shirt off when I get back in the van, and my guys do the same. We'll be ready to meet them in human or wolf form, whichever is required.

We drive another five miles, still climbing the side of a mountain. In the distance, a citadel looms. There's no other word to describe it. Surrounded by smooth adobe walls, an enormous palace sits on a high hill, with balustrade-lined balconies and turrets overlooking the enclave of little thatch-roofed huts below. A medieval-style home to royalty and peasants—that's how it looked.

The road dead-ends at a giant portcullis—closed, of course.

The vans stop, and we start to pile out. A flash of movement coming from behind us makes me whirl and partially shift, but I pull up short.

"Sedona?"

My sister is running at us at top speed. She's wearing some kind of flowy, old-fashioned gown, and I scent her blood, mingled with that of a male's.

Amber was right—not that I doubted it. Sedona's been marked.

"Garrett!" She launches into the air and flies into my arms, wrapping arms and legs around me like a toddler.

I fall back with the impact and hug her. "Sedona. You're all right. We're here now."

When my dad joins us, I put her down, and she hugs him, too.

"How do we get in? I'm going to kill every last motherfucking—"

"*No.*" Sedona shoots a look over her shoulder in the direction she came. A little boy, no more than nine years old, stands there, looking uncertain. "Take me out of here. I don't want a fight. I just want to go home. Let's go."

My dad shakes his head. "No one steals my daughter and lives."

"They didn't steal me, they bought me. You're welcome to kill the fuckers who stole me, but I just want to get out of here. No bloodshed. Let's just leave."

I see my father isn't going for it, so I grab his arm and jerk my head toward the van. "Dad, come here."

His mouth closes in a tight line, but he follows me around the back of the vehicle where we can talk in private. Well, the privacy is largely an illusion because wolves have incredible hearing, but at least the others understand we mean to speak privately.

"Dad, don't you think Sedona's been through enough? She's been *mated*. She might have conflicted feelings toward the guy. The last thing she needs is more trauma. If she says no bloodshed here, I think we have to honor her wishes."

My dad growls.

I hold my ground, refusing to lift my chin or cower to his animal. My wolf is alpha, now. He needs to hear me on this.

"We don't kill them and we send the message we're weak."

"So we come back later and slaughter the whole town," I say drily, although my dad is capable of such violence. "I say for right now, we get Sedona out of here, hear her story, and regroup. If we decide to come back, we come back. I'll gladly rip every last motherfucker limb from limb. You know I will."

The rumble in my father's throat peters out and dies. He gives a single nod and stalks around the van, giving the command to load back up. I blink, somewhat dumbfounded that my father actually let me make the call.

The guys move with military precision, and our caravan is on its way out in less than sixty seconds. I sit in a back seat with Sedona, wrapping an arm around her shoulders and waiting until she's ready to talk.

~.~

WE'RE THREADING through the streets of Mexico City when Sedona finally speaks. "How did you find me?" Despite the ordeal she's been through, she looks vibrant, youth and vitality oozing from her, as if her wolf loved being mated.

"My mate found you." There's so much fucking pride in my voice when I speak, I'm sure Amber can feel my love back in our hotel suite.

I'm coming for you, baby. Almost there.

Sedona lifts weary green eyes. "Your *mate*?"

I touch the back of her neck where her bite marks are healing. "Looks like we both mated this moon."

Sedona's eyes fill with tears, and she looks away. I'm ready to kill the asshole who did this, and I'm dying to get her story, but I force myself to remain silent. If I get aggressive, she'll clam up.

"Tell me about her?" Her voice is choked with tears.

I drop a kiss on the top of her head. "Her name is Amber. She's a human psychic and an attorney. And my next door neighbor. When you went missing, I volun-told her we needed her help, and we brought her along to Mexico. She helped us follow your trail to Mexico City, where we found your captors—they're already dead, by the way—and then she helped get the information on this place."

"A human, huh? Never would've figured." I don't hear a

trace of judgment in Sedona's voice, or I would've gone on the defensive. I'm still expecting more shit from my dad.

"Me, neither." I shrug. "My wolf picked her."

Sedona's face clouds, sadness penetrating her gaze. "Yeah. I guess that happens."

Fuck. She must've fallen for her mate, whoever he is. Could've been Stockholm syndrome.

"You sure you don't want me to go back there and kill the entire Montelobo pack? Because I won't hesitate if you give the word, little sis."

She shakes her head. "I'm sure. Don't let Dad go back, either. I think... they're just a really fucked-up pack." She turns her face up to mine. "So where's Amber, now? When can I meet her?"

I know she's pasting on a sunny face for me, and it kills me. We pull up in front of the hotel. "She's in our suite. Come on. You can meet her now."

We pile out of the van, and I get into the elevator with Sedona, Trey, and Jared. I notice Sedona is quick to join me, just like she was quick to get in my van. She doesn't want to deal with our dad. I don't blame her. I drape an arm over her shoulders, and she leans against me.

I've only been gone six hours, but I'm dying to see Amber. Fates, I hope her bite wound hasn't caused her trouble. She's probably been miserable.

I stick my keycard in the door and swing it open. The moment I do, I know something's wrong.

Amber's scent isn't there. Well, traces are, but she's not in the room. "Amber?" I call out, even so. There's a note on the table, and I snatch it up.

Garrett,

I don't want to bind you to something that happened while under the influence of stress and a full moon. I know that mating with a human will change your position with the pack and with your father, and I don't want to have that weight on my shoulders. Let's write this off as an interesting second date and be done with it.

I caught a plane back to Tucson. Please give me some time before you stop by my apartment—I'd like some distance to heal.

Love,
   Amber

No.

My roar shakes the pictures on the walls. I crumple the note and throw it to the floor.

She can't be gone.

I won't fucking accept it.

I grab my phone and stab in her number before I remember her cell doesn't work here. I let it ring and go to voicemail anyway.

"Amber. I need to talk to you right away. Call me." I want to say a million other things, but I don't trust myself not to fuck it up and say something stupid. Trey, Jarod, and Sedona are all wide-eyed and cautious, staying out of lunging distance but pulling sympathetic faces. "Trey, get Kylie to find out what plane she's on."

"I'm on it, G."

I stalk a tight circle around the room and slam my fist through the wall.

"Garrett," Sedona says sharply.

I swivel to face her, fists clenching. My growls make it hard to hear anything.

"If you want your mate back, you'd better have a better plan than punching holes in plaster."

I blink at her. It takes a full minute for her words to sink in, but then I realize she's right.

"Fuck." I burrow all ten fingers through my hair and hold my head.

I don't have a clue how to win my mate back. Clearly, I had no clue how to court her in the first place, since she said our first two dates were epically bad.

Trey's phone beeps. "You're in luck. She was booked on an early flight out of Mexico City, but she never boarded. She is now rebooked for a flight leaving in"—he looks at his phone–"one hour. Let's go."

I'm relieved to let Trey lead for a moment while my brain tries to rein back my wolf's ferocious desire to reclaim his mate. We all follow him into the elevator and take it down. My dad and some of his pack members are still in the lobby, and they speak to us, but I can't hear for the buzzing in my ears. Somehow they end up joining, too, and we all stream back into one of the vans.

As the vehicle shoots through traffic, my mind plays the reel of every moment I've spent with Amber since the day I met her.

If I'd had any doubt as to why I picked her as a mate, it's clear as day now. A glow pervades every interaction we had. Amber Drake is a gift. To this world. To the kids she helps. To me. She has the heart of an angel and shifter courage. She's delicate but strong. Powerful in her own right. Her capacity to love, to forgive, to offer her time and heart to others knows no bounds.

I need her.

Not just for my wolf. For me.

And I'll do anything in this world to make myself worthy of Amber Drake.

~.~

LET THE RECORD REFLECT: *Breaking up with a wolf causes severe headaches.* I wake up on the floor of the bathroom and find out I missed my flight. I have no idea how long I lay there or if anyone tried to help me.

Women are walking a large circle to avoid going near me, as if whatever knocked me out might be contagious. Heaven forbid someone call 9-1-1. Of course, that number might not work in Mexico.

I drag myself to a ticket counter, rebook for the next flight to the United States, and plunk down to wait. The light from the windows slashes through my head like a physical object. Nausea makes me slightly dizzy.

I can do this. I just need to get home, get into my bed.

Of course that thought reminds me of the last headache I had, when Garrett carried me to my bed and put a cool washcloth on my head. How could I ever have thought of him as a ruffian? He may have a rough exterior, but he's a gentle giant. He never meant to hurt me.

But he has.

Not the bite—I know that will heal. I also know I asked for it.

It's my heart that may never mend.

I went my whole life without ever feeling safe. Or whole.

Or loved. I never belonged, never fit in. With Garrett, all that receded. He embraced all of me—not just Lawyer Amber. He cared about me, about my safety.

But agreeing to mate him after a single weekend together was stupid. It was the equivalent of the drunk Las Vegas wedding at midnight. With or without the Elvis-impersonating preacher. The event you wake up from and realize was a huge mistake.

So I'll go home. Be Lawyer Amber again. Keep helping kids. And, sooner or later, the memories from this weekend will fade.

Right?

I rub my pounding temples and shrink lower in the uncomfortable plastic chair.

A commotion near the security gate forces me to crack one eye to peek, and I go still.

Garrett's marching toward me, flanked by a dozen huge, bad-ass looking men, including Trey, Jared, and his father. Oh, and one female, who must be his sister.

Dark determination scores his face as he eats up the space between us, eyes glued to mine. I brace myself for my headache to increase, for the possibility of passing out again, but it doesn't. Instead, my world goes quiet. All the noise in my head drops back.

I resist the temptation to lean into this. Into Garrett. I left for him. He's better off without me. So I can't let the way my heart flip-flops in my chest, the way my body vibrates with excitement to see him, sway my decision.

We're over.

Garrett comes up so fast and furious, I'm afraid he'll tip out the entire row of chairs I'm sitting in, but he pulls up short when he reaches me. Pulls up short and crouches in front of me.

"Garrett, don't."

"Baby."

Oh God. I didn't count on him speaking so softly, so tenderly. I expected him to throw his weight around with his usual dominant-wolf bullshit. I was prepared to defend my case. But this sweetness knocks me between the eyes, sends a rush of longing and pain to my chest and face that builds, like a pressure cooker.

Garrett clears his throat, as if he's unsure what to say. I'm not used to seeing the cocky wolf so off his game. "I made a lot of mistakes. If I had it to do over, I'd make sure our first and second dates were the best of your life."

Tears swim in my eyes. I blink furiously, not wanting to shed them.

Garrett's entourage has gathered behind him, not offering us any privacy, as if they, too, are a part of this discussion.

"I'd make sure you never doubted the way I feel about you. And I'd make sure you knew it wasn't the full moon or my wolf that picked you for my mate. *I* pick you, Amber Drake. Human. Gifted psychic. Big-hearted lawyer. I need you, baby. And I don't care what any of them think." He finally acknowledges our audience with a jerk of his head. "I don't care if I lose my position as alpha. Or if my family disowns me. All I care about is you. Being with you. Being *for* you.

"Because nothing in my life meant anything until I met you. Now I know my purpose."

So much for not crying. Tears stream down my face as I try not to launch myself into Garrett's arms. "What's that?" I whisper.

"Making myself worthy of you."

"Stop it," I choke.

"I'll shine my shoes and sell the motorcycle, if you want. I'll turn the nightclub over to the guys. I'll help your foster kids. Whatever you need from me, I'm going to be that for you, Amber. Because you're mine. I told you once I marked you, I'd never let you go. And I meant it. But I'm going to work hard for your happiness. I'm going to make you proud to call me your mate.

So much for not launching.

I fly at Garrett, and he catches me. My arms wrap so tight around his neck, I'm strangling him.

"Baby," he croaks. "Is that a *yes*?"

"Yes," I whisper.

The pack gathers around us, into a tight circle. Jared puts a hand on my back, Trey touches Garrett.

Garrett's father clears his throat. "Sounds like Amber's given you the inspiration I never could."

Garrett refuses to release me, whispering unintelligible words into my hair.

"Welcome to the family, Amber," Mr. Green rumbles. "I appreciate what you did to save both my children this weekend."

"Welcome to the pack," Trey and Jarod and many other voices murmur.

Garrett finally releases me, and his sister picks up both my hands and squeezes them. "Thank you for helping them find me," she says. "And welcome to the family."

I remove my hands from her to embrace the beautiful brunette. I sense her own heartbreak as a resonance of what I'd just let go and I want to fix it for her.

"If you'll excuse us." Garrett takes my hand and shoves through the circle. "I need to get my mate back to the hotel." He looks down at me, his eyes soft with affection. "We'll fly home tomorrow. Together. Okay?"

I nod, mutely. I'll have to call work and let them know I'm not coming, but it's fine. I don't have any court appointments.

Garrett sweeps me up in his arms and strides out of the airport, despite my protests.

"Don't worry, Amber. We'll get your luggage," Trey calls after us.

I tuck my face against Garrett's neck. "How did you get past security without a plane ticket?" I ask.

"I don't know. Trey handled it."

Right. He has a pack. My pack, now, too.

~.~

Garrett

I check into a private suite back at the hotel and Jared brings our bags over.

Amber's blushing like a virginal bride, which is the cutest thing I've ever seen. She'll blush even harder when she realizes what I have in store for that hot little body of hers.

"Clothes off." My voice comes out deeper than I expect.

She looks over with lifted brows, probably surprised by the rough command, considering I've been treating her like a delicate flower.

Whatever she sees on my face—must be bald hunger—makes her eyelids droop and nipples peak. She strips out of her clothing.

I rummage through my bag for the duct tape. When I pull it out, she flushes, but her hands go to cup her own breasts, as if I've started an ache there that needs to be relieved.

"Wh-what are you doing?"

I hold up the tape, stalking toward her like a predator sure of his prey. My cock is painfully hard for my new mate. "Since you're having a hard time staying put for me, I thought I'd better secure you."

She licks her pouty lips. "That won't be necessary." Damn, her voice is husky. I fucking love those notes on her. Can't wait to see what else I can coax out of her. I haven't had the time to spend getting to know my mate's body and responses—what makes her quiver, what makes her scream. I sure as hell am going to make up for it now.

I drag a piece of tape out and tear it off. "Oh, I think it's very necessary. You're going to spend all day and night bound to my bed, baby, and maybe then you'll learn to stop running." I rip off a second piece the same length and put them together, sticky side to sticky side. I don't want to hurt my mate's skin tonight. I may like to dominate, but this is definitely all about pleasure.

She lets out a choked laugh. "I'm not run—"

I cut her protest off with a hard kiss at the same time I catch her wrists between us and wrap the tape around them, using a fresh piece to secure it. I slip my finger under the makeshift cuffs to be sure they're snug but not too tight. "That should do." I fold a long piece of tape in half lengthwise and loop it through the cuffs then tug my mate to the bed like a slave with shackles. "On your back to start." I lift my chin toward the mattress.

A tiny smile curls her lips as she climbs up on her knees then settles on her back. I pull her wrists above her head and secure the long piece to the headboard with more duct tape. It wouldn't hold if she really pulled, but this is more about the illusion of capture than the real deal.

I have to stop for a moment and just drink in the sight.

Fucking perfection.

Amber's sweet little body is spread out naked, like an offering, her perky tits falling open to the sides, belly shuddering in when she breathes.

"Open your legs wider, baby."

She inches her thighs apart, a blush creeping up her neck.

I squeeze my cock through my jeans, and groan. "You're so beautiful, Counselor, I can hardly stand it. Even with the full moon behind us."

"Take off your clothes," she orders, eyes dilated, lashes fluttering.

I shake my head. "Nope."

Confusion flits over her face. "Why not?"

"First of all, angel, I call the shots in the bedroom, not you. And you and I both know that's the way you like it, so don't even pretend it's not. Secondly, this is punishment. You left me. I haven't forgotten that. So, you'll lie back and receive whatever I choose to give you, when I choose to give it to you. Understand?"

"N-not really." Her voice wobbles, but I smell her arousal, and the way her chest rises and falls rapidly tells me she's totally turned on by my dictate.

I climb slowly over her, still fully dressed. "Let me explain." I grip her knees and push them up to her shoulders, spreading her wide. I stare down at the pink heart between her thighs, a growl of excitement rumbling from my throat. "I'm going to lick this pretty pussy until I've had my fill. If that takes eighteen hours, and you've screamed yourself hoarse, then maybe you'll learn your lesson."

She laughs that husky laugh that drives me fucking wild.

I let out a snarl and fill my hands with her ass, lift it until her delectable core meets my mouth, and lick into her.

She shudders, knees clamping around my ears. I lick the length of it, part her labia and trace around the insides with the tip of my tongue. Her thighs flex, and she lets out an unsteady moan.

"That's it, beautiful, let me taste what's mine."

I suck her labia, nibble them before applying my tongue to her clit.

Her cries take on a higher pitch—the sound of desperation. I flatten my tongue and lap her from anus to clit, and she starts to pant and moan. I return to her clit and suck while I screw one finger, then two, inside her. The moment I stroke her inner wall, she shatters, her muscles contracting around my fingers, ass squeezing tight, pussy thrusting against my face.

I'm in heaven. Pleasing my female is clearly my purpose in life because I've never felt so powerful.

As soon as she finishes, I start all over again.

I bring her to climax once more. Then go in for a third kill.

She pulls at her bonds. "I can't, Garrett," she moans. "Too much. It's so intense."

"I know, baby. This is punishment. Who do you belong to?" I rim her, licking around her little starfish.

She squeals, clenching her ass, her whole pelvic floor lifting. "You! To Garrett, the most possessive, stubborn, domineering..."

"Uh oh." I laugh. "Someone needs a spanking."

Her pelvic floor contracts again so I know she loves the idea.

I roll her over, adjusting the tape on her wrists to accommodate the new position.

She waggles her ass, inviting my punishment.

I deliver a few swift spanks then rub away the sting. "You know what happens to naughty mates who try to leave the male who marked them?" I reach for one of the pillows and lift her hips, sliding it under.

"Wh-what?"

"They get fucked hard." I spank her again, one smack on each side. "Are you ready for your punishment fuck?"

Her adorable bottom squeezes up tight. "God no." There's a giggle in her voice.

"Too bad, baby. You're going to find out what happens when you displease your mate."

I stretch her ankles wide and use duct tape to fasten each one to the bedposts, again using the method of doubled-up tape so I'm not using the sticky side on her skin.

Her arousal leaks between her thighs, back moves with her panting breath. My female is so excited.

I climb over her and put my lips to her ear. "You know what happens if you're really naughty, baby?"

"What?" Fates, that husky voice. She kills me.

"They get fucked in the ass." I spank her pretty ass a few times. "Do you want me to fuck your tight little ass?"

"No, sir."

My cock jerks. I think it will probably jerk every time she calls me *sir* until the day I die. It's so fucking hot to me when she submits.

I strip out of my clothes and climb up behind Amber, taking a mental picture of the way she looks facedown, spread-eagle, taped to the bed. I file it in the album I hope to soon populate with a million more erotic images: Amber strung up to a hook in the ceiling by her wrists,

Amber leaning backward off the bed to suck my cock, Amber in every yoga position, naked, awaiting my command.

A growl starts to hum in the back of my throat. I fit my cock into the notch between her legs and rub the head in her juices. I slide my cock in slowly, teasing her by taking my time.

She pants, lifting her ass up and tilting her pelvis to give me better access. I sink in deep then draw out, almost all the way.

"No," she whines. "What are you—"

I sink back in.

"Yes. That." She sounds breathless.

I chuckle. "Who's in control here, baby?"

She makes a show of pulling at her restraints. "You are, dammit. Get on with it!"

I pull out and deliver two quick smacks, one to each cheek. "You must want it in the ass today."

"No. No, I don't," she answers quickly, and I laugh again. I grab a pillow and stuff it under her hips to give me a better angle, then I slip in again.

"Oh yes!" she cries out.

I never would've dreamed the uptight lawyer I met the first day would be this expressive. This responsive.

I dip into her again and again, keeping it slow and steady for several strokes. Then my self-control cracks.

"This is when you take it hard, sugar," I warn. I brace my weight on my hands beside her head and plow into her, fucking her deep. If her ankles hadn't been secured, I would've shoved her face all the way up to the headboard, my thrusts were so hard.

Her cries make me crazy, and my wolf goes into a frenzy. I fuck and fuck and fuck her some more, the sound of my loins smacking her ass filling the room, the sound of her cries filling my cars.

"Yes, yes, yes, Garrett!" she screams. Her muscles contract and squeeze in pulses, and I shove in deep to let her enjoy her orgasm. She finishes and goes limp beneath me. I pull out long enough to yank her ankles free then lift her hips until she's on her knees, legs spread wide, ass in the air. Her face still rests on the bed, arms pulled taut over her head.

I slap her pussy. "Did you think we were finished, angel?"

She lets out a long moan. "I can't. Too much...pleasure," she mumbles.

"Oh you will take it, baby. You'll take all the pleasure I want to give you. You know why?"

"Because I'm yours?" There's laughter in her voice.

"That's right. You belong to me. You're mine. Forever." I grip her hips and spear her once more with my cock after taking another mental picture. I slap her pussy again. "Are you ever going to try to leave me again, baby?"

"No, sir."

Three more spanks right over her clit.

She moans.

"Naughty baby. Now I have to fuck you until you're delirious."

"I already am." Her words are muffled by the covers and possibly slurred with lust.

I lean down to flick my tongue over her moist folds.

"Oh God," she groans.

I may want to torture my mate with multiple orgasms, but my endurance won't last much longer. I stand on my knees behind her and line my cock up with her entrance. I sink into her moist heat and groan. It's even better from this angle. Fingers tight around her hips, I pump into her, own her sweet body, command it. My eyeballs flip back in my head. She feels too good. Too tight. Too hot. Too right.

My climax comes on like a freight train, barrels through me. I choke on a curse and fuck her right through it, plowing her as ribbons of cum erupt from my cock.

Time becomes slippery. I don't know how long it's been when my vision clears and I realize I've stopped fucking my new mate. I'm still pinned to her backside, balls deep inside her. My breath scrapes in and out like I've run a marathon.

Amber moans softly, a contented sound, and nuzzles the blankets. I rip the duct tape cuffs from her wrists and pull her to her side so I can curl up around her. She fits beside me like our bodies were made to nest together.

I stroke her hair back from her face. "You okay?"

She nods, a dreamy expression softening her mouth into a smile.

"How was that for a third date?"

"Mmm." She reaches up and touches my face. "Epic."

EPILOGUE

Amber

The sign outside Eclipse reads *Closed for Private Event*. Inside, kids run through Garrett's club. It took a while to get them warmed up. Most foster kids have been through ugly situations. They aren't carefree. They hold back.

But when Garrett runs to the face-painting booth and shouts, "Face-painting is cool. Can I get a wolf?" it warms the kids up. The giant, tattooed tough guy modeling the wolf convinces every kid to get one just like it.

Watching him, my heart is full to the point of bursting. He has more than honored his promise of making himself worthy for me, not that I thought he wasn't before. No, his clothes haven't changed, and he still rides a motorcycle, but he takes steps every day to make our future beautiful. Like getting the plans drawn up for our dream house. And taking me on real dates.

"Alisa, are you going to get a Shirley Temple?" I ask the

shy redhead who just went through the system with me as her representative.

Her wide green eyes lock on my face, but she doesn't answer, which is pretty typical.

"It's a drink. Sam is making them over there." I point toward the bar where the young werewolf is mixing kid drinks.

Her new adoptive mom picks up her hand. "Do you want to try one?"

She nods, still staring at me.

"I'll give you a tip—tell them you want extra cherries." I wink and she smiles, revealing huge gaps where her baby teeth have fallen out.

"Who knows how to do the Cupid Shuffle?" Jared calls out. He's playing both DJ and dance coach out on the dance floor, with Trey as his backup. They're in the midst of the kids, shaking it with them in the mini light show.

The strains of "Cupid Shuffle" come on, and Jared takes a spot in the front of the group, leading them right and left, kicking and turning.

I'm smiling like a goofball, so touched at how generous Garrett and his pack are with these kids, who aren't even shifters.

They're good people. Wolves.

And I'm so honored to be included in their midst.

~.~

MUCH LATER, I press into Garrett's solid, warm body as he motors up the mountain. The city has a light ordinance to keep it dark for the telescopes on Kitt Peak; few artificial lights compete with the night sky. A few months ago, I would've thought it was too dangerous to ride at night, but holding tight to Garrett, feeling his rock-hard muscles flex against my arms, I've never felt more safe.

The bike purrs off the road to an overlook. Garrett parks it and pulls me in front of him. We sit together and watch the show.

"That was a great thing you did today, opening up the club to the kids," I murmur. "I didn't know you were so good with kids."

"I didn't, either," he chuckles.

"Well, you were awesome."

"Am I going to get a reward?" He shifts me on his lap, and I feel just what sort of reward he wants.

"Mmm," I stroke his rigid length under his jeans. "Maybe later."

"Not here?"

I laugh. "I'm not quite that wild, yet."

He kisses me, a deep, drawn-out kiss that has me moaning in my throat.

"How about now?"

"Bad boy." I shift on the bike so I'm straddling his lap, facing him. The view is so beautiful, but I only want to look at him.

He threads his fingers through my hair. I wear it down most days, now. It's crazy tangled from the wind, but he seems to like it.

For a second his face blurs. I see Garrett, a little older and looking like his dad, in the driveway of an adobe brick home. Three kids—a girl and two boys—run and play around him as he fixes his motorcycle, sometimes stopping to show them how to turn a wrench.

As the vision fades, I hug him close.

"Do you want kids?" I blurt.

A chuckle rumbles through him. "Not sure how great a dad I'll be, but yes. Though I was hoping for more time alone with you before we add some rug rats."

"Rug wolves? We can always get Jared or Trey to babysit."

"Or lock the bedroom door."

"That only works if you don't teach them how to pick locks," I scold, and he laughs, shifting me back so he can see my face.

"What's all this talk about kids? Are you..." The hopeful tone of his voice tells me all I need to know.

"No. I don't think so." *Not yet,* I add silently, tracing the scruff on his chin. "I just had a vision of the future."

"Really? What was it?"

I smile. "You'll find out."

∽

~Check out the deleted scenes from *Alpha's Danger*~
https://instafreebie.com/free/HcXeO

EXCERPT: ALPHA'S PRIZE

Please enjoy this short excerpt from the next book in the *Bad Boy Alphas* Series

Alpha's Prize - Excerpt

Sedona

My eyes crack open. They're gritty and sore. I'd rub them if I weren't in wolf form.

Where am I?

I attempt to move and hit against metal bars. *Oh fates.* I'm in a cage—a *fucking cage*.

It all floods back to me. I was on my morning run on the beach in San Carlos. Spring break in Mexico. I caught the scent of a male shifter, and I stopped, turning in a slow circle to identify where it was coming from. A guy lifts his hand in a wave. He walks over, casual-like, but the hairs on the back of my neck are standing up.

I know he's going to be a problem.

I also think I have a good chance of taking him. I'm the daughter of an alpha. I'm twenty-one years old—young. Fit. Ready.

The guy walks up with a friendly smile in place. He's saying something in Spanish.

I start to tell him, *No hablo*, when something mother-fucking sharp jabs in my neck from behind. I shift, out of fear and necessity. My wolf wants to protect me. My tank and jogging shorts tear as I change shape, but my legs won't hold. I'm down on my side in the sand, my white fur too hot in the sun. Above me, five men stand in a circle, peering down.

It goes fuzzy from there. I remember being put in the cage, and the cage being put in the baggage compartment of a commercial plane. Like I'm a fucking dog or something. Someone's goddamn pet.

Fuck.

My head aches, and I have a serious case of cotton-mouth. Like worse than any hangover I've had in the last three years of college. Not that I'm a party girl or anything.

Well, sometimes I like to party, but who doesn't?

I twist in the confined space, but it's impossible to get comfortable. A low growl starts in my throat, and my wolf hunches down like she's going to pounce, even though there's no way out of this damn cage. I know because I now remember waking up on previous occasions and trying. Jesus. How long have I been floating in and out of consciousness? Twelve hours? Twenty-four?

It looks like I'm in a large warehouse. There are other cages lining a giant metal rack of shelves—like the kind products are stored on in Costco or Sam's Club. Most are empty. A skinny black wolf with yellow eyes blinks at me from where he lies on his side in one of them.

Cigar smoke tinges the air and the sound of men's voices, speaking in Spanish, comes from behind a door.

I remember throwing up in my cage from the bumpy ride here, or maybe just from the drugs. Someone cleaned me up afterward, speaking softly in Spanish, as if trying to soothe me. I bared my teeth and tried to take his hand off, but he jabbed another needle into my neck, and I fell back into the heavy slumber.

The door swings open, allowing a shaft of light to fall from the corridor. The masculine voices draw nearer until a group of men gather around my cage. The same assholes who grabbed me on the beach.

If I were smart, I'd shift and get some information out of them. Who they are, what they want with me. But my wolf isn't having any talking.

I surge to my feet, slamming my back and head against the top wires, the prison too small to contain me, standing. My lips peel back to show my fangs, and the growl starting low in my throat is deadly.

"*Que belleza, no?*" one of the men asks.

They're wolves, judging by their scent. All of them. And the way they leer at me sends a cold prickle of fear through me.

I snap my jaws through the wires, snarling.

Ignoring me, the men pick up my cage and carry me outside to a gleaming white passenger van. The men open the back doors of the van and lift me inside.

I throw myself against the wires of the cage, barking and growling.

One of the men chuckles. "*Tranquila, angel, tranquila.*" He swings the doors shut with a decisive click, leaving me alone once more.

Alpha's Prize (coming soon!)

MY CAPTIVE. MY MATE. MY PRIZE.

I didn't order the capture of the beautiful American she-wolf. I didn't buy her from the traffickers. I didn't even plan to claim her. But no male shifter could have withstood the test of a full moon and a locked room with Sedona, naked and shackled to the bed.

I lost control, not only claiming her, but also marking her, and leaving her pregnant with my wolfpup. I won't keep her prisoner, as much as I'd like to. I allow her to escape to the safety of her brother's pack.

But once marked, no she-wolf is ever really free. I will follow her to the ends of the Earth, if I must.

Sedona belongs to me.

ACKNOWLEDGMENTS

Thank you to Aubrey Cara, Katherine Deane and Margarita for their beta reads! Thank you to Margarita for the contract.

ABOUT RENEE ROSE

USA TODAY BESTSELLING AUTHOR RENEE ROSE is a naughty wordsmith who writes kinky romance novels. Named Eroticon USA's Next Top Erotic Author in 2013, she has also won *The Romance Reviews* Best Historical Romance, and *Spanking Romance Reviews'* Best Historical, Best Erotic, Best Ageplay and favorite author. She's hit #1 on Amazon in the Erotic Paranormal, Western and Sci-fi categories. She also pens BDSM stories under the name Darling Adams.

Renee loves to connect with readers! Please visit her on:
    Blog | Twitter | Facebook | Goodreads | Pinterest | Instagram

Want FREE Renee Rose books?
    Go to http://owned.gr8.com to sign up for Renee Rose's newsletter and receive a free copy of *Theirs to Protect, Owned by the Marine, Theirs to Punish, The Alpha's Punishment, Disobedience at the Dressmaker's* and *Her Billionaire Boss*. In addition to the free stories, you will also get special pricing, exclusive previews and news of new releases.

CHECK OUT RENEE'S ZANDIAN MASTERS SERIES!

HIS HUMAN SLAVE - EXCERPT

CHAPTER ONE

Zandian Breeding season.

That was the last consideration in his mind before liberating his planet from the Finn.

Breeding season.

Zander sat at the round platform, looking at the faces of the elders he respected most, the ones who had risked their lives to save him when the Finn invaded Zandia and wiped out the rest of their species solar cycles before.

"You can't be serious."

"Dead serious," Daneth, the only Zandian physician left in the galaxy said, tapping his wrist band. "You are the best male representative of the Zandian species, the only one left of the royal bloodline, and, more importantly, the only one young enough to produce healthy offspring. If you go to battle without first procreating, our species will die with us."

He gestured around the room at the other members of his parents' generation.

He leaned back in his chair and closed his eyes in exasperation. "And exactly which female do you think I will produce these offspring with? Last I heard, there is no Zandian female under the age of sixty left alive."

"You will have to cross-breed. I purchased a program and entered your genetic makeup. It uses all the known gene files in the galaxy predicts the best possible mate for breeding.

He raised his eyebrows. "So have you already run this program?"

Daneth nodded.

He looked around the table, his gaze resting on Seke, his arms master and war strategist. "Did you know about this?"

Seke nodded once.

"And you approve? This is foolish—my time should be spent training with the new battleships we bought and recruiting an army, not—" he spluttered to a stop.

"The continuation of the species is paramount. What is the point of winning back Zandia if there's no Zandians left to populate it?"

He sighed, blowing out his breath. "All right, I'll bite. Who is she? What species?"

Daneth projected an image from his wrist band. The image of a slight, tawny-haired young female appeared. "Human. Lamira Taniaka. She's an Ocretion slave working in agrifarming."

A human breeder. A slave.

Veck.

Zander didn't have time for this excrement. "There's been a miscalculation." He waved his hand at the hologram.

"No, no mistake. I ran the program several times. This

female bested every other candidate by at least a thousand metapoints. This female will produce the most suitable offspring for you."

"Impossible. Not a human. No." Humans were the lowest of the social strata on Ocretia, the planet where his palatial pod had been granted airspace.

"I realize it seems an unlikely match, my lord, but there must be some reason her genes mix best with yours. The program is flawless."

"I thought you might suggest someone worthy of formal mating—an arranged marriage with royalty of another species. Not a breeder. Not a *pet.*" Humans were not mates, they were slaves to the Ocretions. An inferior species. He hadn't had much to do with them, but from what he understood, they were weak, fragile. Their lifespan was short, they did not recover from injuries quickly. They spread disease and died quickly. They lacked honor and fortitude. They lied.

Zandians—his species—never lied.

"I was not seeking a lifemate for you, I found the best female for producing your offspring. If you wish to find a mate, I will search the databases for the female most compatible to your personality and lifestyle preferences after you have bred. But this is the one you must breed. And now, during the traditional Zandian breeding season."

He closed his eyes and shook his head. The breeding season didn't matter. For one thing, they weren't on Zandia —weren't affected by her moons, or her atmosphere. For another, he wouldn't be breeding with a Zandian female coming into cycle.

But Daneth was like a sharkhound on a hunt—he wouldn't stop until the stated goal had been reached. He'd been his father's physician and had served on Zander's council as a trusted advisor since the day they'd evacuated Zandia during the Finn's takeover. He'd been only fourteen sun-cycles then. He'd spent the last fifteen sun-cycles working every day on his plan to retake his planet. He'd settled in Ocretia where he'd amassed a small fortune through business and trade, making connections and preparing resources, training for war.

"I will take care of everything. I will purchase her and bring her here until you impregnate her. Once it's done, you can send her away. I'm certain you'll be satisfied with the results. The program is never wrong."

"She's human. And a slave. You know I don't believe in keeping slaves."

"So set her free when she's served you." Lium, his tactical engineer spoke.

"A slave will have to be imprisoned. Guarded. Disciplined."

"She's beautiful. Would it be such a hardship to have this woman chained in your bedroom?" This from Erick, his trade and business advisor.

Beautiful? He looked again at the holograph. The female looked filthy, with dirt covering her hands and cheeks, her unkempt hair pulled back and secured at her nape. But upon closer inspection, it seemed Erick was right. She was pretty—for a human. Her tangled hair was an unusual copper color and wide-set green eyes blinked at the imager that had captured her likeness. A smattering of light freckles dusted her golden skin. She wore drab shapeless work garments, but when Daneth hit a command to remove the clothing and predict the shape of her naked body, it appeared to be in perfect proportion—round, firm breasts, wide hips, long, muscular legs. His horns and cock stiffened in unison.

Veck.

He hadn't had that reaction to a female of another species before. He'd only grown hard looking at old holograms of naked or scantily clad Zandian females from the archives.

For the love of Zandia.

He didn't want a human. He wanted the impossible—one of his own species, or if not, then a female of a species that was superior to his own, not inferior.

"Why do you suppose her genes are best? What else do you know about her?"

"Well, there's this." Daneth flashed up a holograph of a human man, dressed in combat gear, a lightray gun in his hand, blood dripping from his forehead. "He was her father, a rebel warrior who fought in the last human uprising before her birth. He may have even led it."

"Hmm." He made a noncommittal sound. His species were warriors, why would he need the human genome for that? "What about her mother?"

"Not much to be found. She's still alive—they're together now, working on Earth-based plant and food growth production. Keeping their heads down, is my guess. The data about her father isn't in the Ocretion database file. My program gene-matched to give me that information. I'm surprised the Ocretions don't do more gene study."

"I'll probably split her in two the first time I use her. Humans aren't not built for Zandian cocks."

"The program can't be wrong."

He sighed. "Is she even for sale?"

"No, but you are a highly-esteemed royalty and unofficial ambassador from Zandia. I'm sure she can be purchased for the right price." Daneth referred to his position on the United Galaxies. Since the Finns were not recognized by the

UG due to their genocidal practices, Zander served as the Zandian ambassador. Not that it did much good. No one on the UG was willing to put their resources behind him to overthrow the Finns.

He made a grumbling sound in his throat. "Fine. But don't spend too much. Our resources are needed for recruiting soldiers."

"Your offspring are top priority. Even over the war plans," Seke said. The male didn't speak often, and when he did, it always had a definitive ring to it, as if his word was the last and only word.

"As you wish. I'll breed her. But if she doesn't survive the first coupling, her death is on all of you."

Daneth chuckled. "Humans aren't that weak."

~.~

Lamira crouched beside the row of tomato plants and flicked a bug off the leaf before anyone saw it. The Ocretion foremen always wanted to spray the plants with their chemicals at the first sign of any bugs, even though it had been proven to harm the plants.

Her stomach rumbled. The tomatoes looked so juicy. She longed to just pluck one and pop it into her mouth, but she'd never get away with it. She'd be publicly flogged or worse—shocked. The fresh Earth-based fruits and vegetables they cultivated were only for Ocretions. Human slaves had to live on packaged food that wasn't fit for a dog.

Still, her life was far better than it might be in another sector, as her mother always reminded her. They lived in their own tent and had little contact with their owners after work hours.

It might be worse. She could be a sex slave like the sister she'd never met, her body used and abused by men every day. After the Ocretions took her sister, her father had led a human uprising, which had resulted in his death. Her mother, pregnant with Lamira, had been picked up by slave smugglers and sold to the agrifarm. Her mother had been careful to hide her beauty and taught her to do the same, keeping mud on her face and hair and wearing clothes that were too big. They hunched when they walked, ducked their heads when addressed, and kept their eyes lowered. Only in their own ragged tent did they relax.

"You, there—Lamira." A guard called her name.

She hunched her shoulders and looked up.

"The director wants to see you."

Her heart thudded in her chest. What had she done? She was careful, always careful. By the age of seven her mother had taught her to distinguish what was real—what others knew—and what was claircognizance. She'd learned to keep her mouth shut for fear she'd slip up and say something she knew about someone without having been told. Had she made a mistake? If she had, it would mean certain death. Humans with special traits—anything abnormal or special—were exterminated. The Ocretions wanted a population they could easily control.

She dropped the bushel of tomatoes and walked up to the main building, showing the barcode on her wrist to the scanner to gain admittance. She'd never been in the administration building before. An unimpressive concrete slab, it felt as cold and dreary inside as it looked from the outside. One of the guards jerked his head. "Director's office is that way."

The gray concrete floors chilled her dirty bare feet. The director was a fat, pasty Ocretion female with ears that stuck straight out to the sides and cheeks as paunchy as her belly. Beside her sat a male of a species she didn't recognize.

"Lamira." The director said her name, but didn't follow with any instructions.

She stood there, not sure what to do. She tried for a curtsy.

The humanoid male stood up and circled her. He appeared middle-aged and stood a head taller than a human, but unlike the doughy Ocretions, he was all lean muscle. Two small horns or antennae protruded from his head. "She's in good health?"

The director shrugged, looking bored. "I wouldn't know."

The male lifted her hair to peer under her ponytail. He lifted her arms and palpated her armpits. His skin was purplish-peach, a nice hue—an almost human color. His interest in her seemed clinical, not sexual, more like a doctor or scientist.

"What is this about?" she asked.

The male raised an eyebrow, as if surprised she'd spoken.

The director touched the fingertips of her four-fingered hands together. "They are not house-trained, the humans we keep here. They're mainly used for outdoor agricultural work."

House-trained. What in the stars did that mean?

He cupped her breasts and squeezed them.

She jerked back in shock.

"Stand still, human," the director barked, picking up her shock-stick and sauntering over.

Lamira froze and held her breath. She hated the shock-stick more than any other punishment. She'd heard if you get shocked enough, permanent paralysis or even death may result. In her case, she feared she might say something she shouldn't while coming out of the daze from it.

"I'll take her. We'll require a full examination to ensure her good health, of course, but if everything seems in order, I will pay for her."

The director folded her arms across her chest. "Well, we weren't planning to sell her. I understand Prince Zander has a lot of influence with the United Galaxies, but—"

"Two hundred steins."

Her breath caught. Surely they weren't negotiating for *her*—for her life? What about her mother? Her plants? She couldn't leave.

"Three hundred fifty."

Her head swam and she swayed on her feet. No. This couldn't be happening. Her claircognizance should have warned her about this, but it never worked in her favor— just told her meaningless things about other people. A true curse.

"Done." The male punched something into his wrist-band and a beep sounded on the director's hand held communication device.

The director looked down at it and smiled. "When do you want her?"

The male gripped her upper arm. "I'll take her now." He bowed. "It was nice doing business with you."

She swung around to meet him, terror screaming in her chest. "I can't—wait—"

The male ignored her, pressing a device to the back of her neck.

She felt a sting before everything went black.

HIS HUMAN SLAVE (Book One)

COLLARED AND CAGED, HIS HUMAN SLAVE AWAITS HER TRAINING.

Zander, the alien warrior prince intent on recovering his planet, needs a mate. While he would never choose a human of his own accord, his physician's gene-matching program selected Lamira's DNA as the best possible match with his own. Now he must teach the beautiful slave to yield to his will, accept his discipline and learn to serve him as her one true master.

Lamira has hidden her claircognizance from the Ocretions, as aberrant traits in human slaves are punished by death. When she's bought by a Zandian prince for breeding and kept by his side at all times, she finds it increasingly harder to hide. His humiliating punishments and dominance awake a powerful lust in her, which he tracks with a monitoring device on her arousal rate. But when she begins to care for the huge, demanding alien, she must choose between preserving her own life and revealing her secret to save his.

OTHER TITLES BY RENEE ROSE

Paranormal

Bad Boy Alphas Series

Alpha's Danger

Alpha's Temptation

Love in the Elevator (Bonus story to Alpha's Temptation)

Alpha Doms Series

The Alpha's Hunger,

The Alpha's Promise,

The Alpha's Punishment,

Other Books set in the world of Bad Boy Alphas

His Captive Mortal

Deathless Love

Deathless Discipline

The Winter Storm: An Ever After Chronicle

Sci-Fi

Zandian Masters Series

His Human Slave

His Human Prisoner

Training His Human

His Human Rebel

His Human Vessel

His Mate and Master

Zandian Pet (coming soon!)

The Hand of Vengeance

Her Alien Masters

Dark Mafia Romance

The Russian, *The Don's Daughter*, *Mob Mistress*, *The Bossman*

Contemporary

Her Royal Master (Royally Mine), *The Russian (Hero Undercover)*, *Black Light: Valentine Roulette*, *Theirs to Protect*, *Scoring with Santa*, *Owned by the Marine*, *Theirs to Punish*, *Punishing Portia*, *The Professor's Girl*, *Safe in his Arms*, *Saved*, *The Elusive "O"*

Regency

The Darlington Incident, *Humbled*, *The Reddington Scandal*, *The Westerfield Affair*, *Pleasing the Colonel*

Western

His Little Lapis, *The Devil of Whiskey Row*, *The Outlaw's Bride*

Medieval

Mercenary, *Medieval Discipline*, *Lords and Ladies*, *The Knight's Prisoner*, *Betrothed*, *Held for Ransom*, *The Knight's Seduction*, *The Conquered Brides (5 book box set)*

Renaissance

Renaissance Discipline

Ageplay

Stepbrother's Rules, *Her Hollywood Daddy*, *His Little Lapis*, *Black Light: Valentine's Roulette (Broken)*

BDSM under the name Darling Adams

Medical Play

Yes, Doctor,

Master/Slave

Punishing Portia

ABOUT LEE SAVINO

Lee Savino is a USA today bestselling author, mom and choco-holic.

Warning: Do not read her Berserker series, or you will be addicted to the huge, dominant warriors who will stop at nothing to claim their mates.

I repeat: Do. Not. Read. The Berserker Saga. Particularly not the thrilling excerpt below.

Download a free book from www.leesavino.com (don't read that, either. Too much hot sexy lovin').

EXCERPT: SOLD TO THE BERSERKERS BY LEE SAVINO

Sold to the Berserkers

A ménage shifter romance

By Lee Savino

CHAPTER ONE

The day my stepfather sold me to the Berserkers, I woke at dawn with him leering over me. "Get up." He made to kick me and I scrambled out of my sleep stupor to my feet.

"I need your help with a delivery."

I nodded and glanced at my sleeping mother and siblings. I didn't trust my stepfather around my three younger sisters, but if I was gone with him all day, they'd be safe. I'd taken to carrying a dirk myself. I did not dare kill him; we needed him for food and shelter, but if he attacked me again, I would fight.

My mother's second husband hated me, ever since the last time he'd tried to take me and I had fought back. My mother was gone to market, and when he tried to grab me, something in me snapped. I would not let him touch me again. I fought, kicking and scratching, and finally grabbing an iron pot and scalding him with heated water.

He bellowed and looked as if he wanted to hurt me, but kept his distance. When my mother returned he pretended like nothing was wrong, but his eyes followed me with hatred and cunning.

Out loud he called me ugly and mocking the scar that marred my neck since a wild dog attacked me when I was young. I ignored this and kept my distance. I'd heard the taunts about my hideous face since the wounds had healed into scars, a mass of silver tissue at my neck.

That morning, I wrapped a scarf over my hair and scarred neck and followed my stepfather, carrying his wares down the old road. At first I thought we were headed to the great market, but when we reached the fork in the road and he went an unfamiliar way, I hesitated. Something wasn't right.

"This way, cur." He'd taken to calling me "dog". He'd taunted me, saying the only sounds I could make were grunts like a beast, so I might as well be one. He was right. The attack had taken my voice by damaging my throat.

If I followed him into the forest and he tried to kill me, I wouldn't even be able to cry out.

"There's a rich man who asked for his wares delivered to his door." He marched on without a backward glance and I followed.

I had lived all my life in the kingdom of Alba, but when my father died and my mother remarried, we moved to my stepfather's village in the highlands, at the foot of the great, forbidding mountains. There were stories of evil that lived in the dark crevices of the heights, but I'd never believed them.

I knew enough monsters living in plain sight.

The longer we walked, the lower the sun sank in the sky, the more I knew my stepfather was trying to trick me, that there was no rich man waiting for these wares.

When the path curved, and my stepfather stepped out from behind a boulder to surprise me, I was half ready, but before I could reach for my dirk he struck me so hard I fell.

I woke tied to a tree.

The light was lower, heralding dusk. I struggled silently, frantic gasps escaping from my scarred throat. My stepfather stepped into view and I felt a second of relief at a familiar face, before remembering the evil this man had wrought on my body. Whatever he was planning, it would bode ill for me, and my younger sisters. If I didn't survive, they would eventually share the same fate as mine.

"You're awake," he said. "Just in time for the sale."

I strained but my bonds held fast. As my stepfather approached, I realized that the scarf that I wrapped around my neck to hide my scars had fallen, exposing them. Out of habit, I twitched my head to the side, tucking my bad side towards my shoulder.

My stepfather smirked.

"So ugly," he sneered. "I could never find a husband for you, but I found someone to take you. A group of warriors passing through who saw you, and want to slake their lust on your body. Who knows, if you please them, they may let you live. But I doubt you'll survive these men. They're foreigners, mercenaries, come to fight for the king. Berserkers. If you're lucky your death will be swift when they tear you apart."

I'd heard the tales of berserker warriors, fearsome

warriors of old. Ageless, timeless, they'd sailed over the seas to the land, plundering, killing, taking slaves, they fought for our kings, and their own. Nothing could stand in their path when they went into a killing rage.

I fought to keep my fear off my face. Berserker's were a myth, so my stepfather had probably sold me to a band of passing soldiers who would take their pleasure from my flesh before leaving me for dead, or selling me on.

"I could've sold you long ago, if I stripped you bare and put a bag over you head to hide those scars."

His hands pawed at me, and I shied away from his disgusting breath. He slapped me, then tore at my braid, letting my hair spill over my face and shoulders.

Bound as I was, I still could glare at him. I could do nothing to stop the sale, but I hoped my fierce expression told him I'd fight to the death if he tried to force himself on me.

His hand started to wander down towards my breast when a shadow moved on the edge of the clearing. It caught my eye and I startled. My stepfather stepped back as the warriors poured from the trees.

My first thought was that they were not men, but beasts. They prowled forward, dark shapes almost one with the shadows. A few wore animal pelts and held back, lurking on the edge of the woods. Two came forward, wearing the garb of warriors, bristling with weapons. One had dark hair, and the other long, dirty blond with a beard to match.

Their eyes glowed with a terrifying light.

As they approached, the smell of raw meat and blood wafted over us, and my stomach twisted. I was glad my stepfather hadn't fed me all day, or I would've emptied my guts on the ground.

My stepfather's face and tone took on the wheedling expression I'd seen when he was selling in the market.

"Good evening, sirs," he cringed before the largest, the blond with hair streaming down his chest.

They were perfectly silent, but the blond approached, fixing me with strange golden eyes.

Their faces were fair enough, but their hulking forms and the quick, light way they moved made me catch my breath. I had never seen such massive men. Beside them, my stepfather looked like an ugly dwarf.

"This is the one you wanted," my stepfather continued. "She's healthy and strong. She will be a good slave for you."

My body would've shaken with terror, if I were not bound so tightly.

A dark haired warrior stepped up beside the blond and the two exchanged a look.

"You asked for the one with scars." My stepfather took my hair and jerked my head back, exposing the horrible, silvery mass. I shut my eyes, tears squeezing out at the sudden pain and humiliation.

The next thing I knew, my stepfather's grip loosened. A grunt, and I opened my eyes to see the dark haired warrior standing at my side. My stepfather sprawled on the ground as if he'd been pushed.

The blond leader prodded a boot into my stepfather's side.

"Get up," the blond said, in a voice that was more a growl than a human sound. It curdled my blood. My stepfather scrambled to his feet.

The black haired man cut away the last of my bonds, and I sagged forward. I would've fallen but he caught me easily and set me on my feet, keeping his arms around me. I was not the smallest woman, but he was a giant. Muscles bulged in his arms and chest, but he held me carefully. I stared at him, taking in his raven dark hair and strange gold eyes.

He tucked me closer to his muscled body.

Meanwhile, my stepfather whined. "I just wanted to show you the scars—"

Again that frightening growl from the blond. "You don't touch what is ours."

"I don't want to touch her." My stepfather spat.

Despite myself, I cowered against the man who held me. A stranger I had never met, he was still a safer haven than my stepfather.

"I only wish to make sure you are satisfied, milords. Do you want to sample her?" my stepfather asked in an evil tone. He wanted to see me torn apart.

A growl rumbled under my ear and I lifted my head. Who were these men, these great warriors who had bought and paid for me? The arms around my body were strong and solid, inescapable, but the gold eyes looking down at me were kind. The warrior ran his thumb across the pad of my lips, and his fingers were gentle for such a large, violent looking warrior. Under the scent of blood, he smelled of snow and sharp cold, a clean scent.

He pressed his face against my head, breathing in a deep breath.

The blond was looking at us.

"It's her," the black haired man growled, his voice so guttural. "This is the one."

One of his hands came to cover the side of my face and throat, holding my face to his chest in a protective gesture.

I closed my eyes, relaxing in the solid warmth of the warrior's body.

A clink of gold, and the deed was done. I'd been sold.

ALMOST IMMEDIATELY, the warrior started pulling me away.

I fought my rising panic, wishing that my stepfather's was not the last familiar face I saw.

"Goodbye, Brenna," my stepfather smirked as the warriors streamed past him, following their blond leader into the forest.

"Wait," the blond stopped. Immediately the warriors grabbed my stepfather. "Her name is Brenna?"

"Yes. But you bought her. Call her what you like."

The dark haired warrior tugged me on. I half followed, half staggered along beside him. My nails bit into my palms so I could keep myself from panicking. Fighting the giant beside me wasn't an option. Neither was trying to outrun him.

The blond joined us, and the two warriors pulled me into the dark grove. Terrible thoughts poured into my mind. I belonged to these men, and now they would rape me, sate themselves with my body, then cut my throat and leave me for the wolves.

My eyes filled with tears, both angry and frightened.

They stopped as one and drew me between them. I shut my eyes in defiance, and the tears leaked out.

As I healed from the attack, I could make some noises, horrible, animal things, but they were so ugly, I stopped making any sounds at all. Sometimes, when alone, I'd sink into the river, open my mouth and try to scream. But no sound came out anymore. My throat had forgotten my voice.

Now the only sound in the grove was my harsh breathing.

I sensed the warriors on either side of me, their massive

shapes towering over my fragile body. I was much smaller than them, tiny and petite beside their massive forms.

Right now I tried to remember to breathe and submit to these men. One blow and they could kill me.

My heart beat so hard it was painful. I was ready to die.

But when they touched me they were gentle. A hand brushed back my hair, then stroked my jaw. One steadied me from behind as the other cupped my head and turned my head this way and that. The one behind me gathered my hair behind me. I held my breath as the two massive warriors handled me.

I realized the smell of blood had fallen away, replaced by another scent, an animal musk that was much more pleasant.

A finger ran over my neck, near the scar and I sucked in a breath. The hands dropped away.

Their faces dipped close to mine, and I felt their breath on my skin as if they took deep scents of my hair.

"So good," one of them groaned.

I didn't understand. I was afraid of them taking me but I didn't know why they weren't.

"It's working," one murmured to the other. "The witch was right."

As they dipped their heads and scented me, my heart beat faster in response to their proximity. Something stirred deep inside me. Desire. A few minutes alone with these men and I'd been more intimate with them than any other.

As one they bent their heads to mine, nuzzling close to my neck a tingling spread over my skin.

I felt it then, unbidden, a stirring in my loins. Ever since I had come into womanhood, my desires were strong. Every month I fought the pull to find a man and join with him. I was hideous and destined to be an outcast and alone. But each full moon my body came alive, beset by waves of roiling lust until I felt desperate enough to grab the nearest man and beg him to give me sons.

The heat poured over me until I heard a gasp—one of the warriors jerked back and stepped away.

"She's ready," one growled. Instead of frightening, the sound excited me.

What was happening?

"Not here, brother," the blond rasped.

Without answering, the dark-haired one pulled me on.

For a while we walked, pushing through the forest and forded a stream. The heat in me faded as I followed, weak with hunger and fear, eventually stumbling on exhaustion numbed feet.

The dark-haired warrior stopped, and I flinched, expecting him to bully me into continuing on.

Instead, he guided me to face him. Again his hands came to me, stroking back my hair. I winced when I realized what he was doing: looking at my scar.

Involuntarily my head jerked and he let my chin go, offering me water instead. He held the skin while I drank, and when I'd had my fill he offered me dried meat, feeding me from his hand. I stared into the strange golden eyes, unable to keep the questions off my face: Who are you? What are you going to do with me?

When I was done, he lay a hand on his chest and uttered a guttural sound I didn't understand. He repeated it twice, then lay his hand on my chest.

"Brenna." I could barely make out my name, but I nodded.

A shadow of a smile curved his full lips. Shrugging off the gray pelt he wore, he wrapped it around my shoulders before pulling me back into the circle of his strong arms.

My heart beat faster. The pelt's warmth seeped into my tired body, and the big man held me steady. I still felt frightened, but waited obediently in the dark haired warrior's embrace. I dared not struggle.

The brush around us rippled and the warriors surrounded us. I shrank towards my black-haired captor, but he held me fast, turning me so I faced the warrior who seemed to be their leader.

The blond was so huge, my neck had to tip back to see him. He moved forward and I couldn't help trembling so hard I would've fallen if the dark haired warrior let me go. Every instinct in me screamed that this was a wild man, a beast a dangerous monster and I needed to run.

He reached out and I flinched.

His hand halted.

He swallowed, as if trying to remember how to use his voice.

"Brenna." My name was no more than a soft growl. "We mean you no harm."

I studied him. As big as the warriors were, the blond was one of the largest. He walked lightly, muscles bulging. Long locks of blond hair brushed his broad shoulders. His face was rawboned and half covered in a beard, the defining feature his great gold eyebrows over those amazing eyes.

When his gaze caught mine, his eyes glowed.

His hands touched my face, a thumb stroking my lips. He tilted it to and fro. He pushed my hair away from my neck. I shut my eyes, knowing what he saw, the white weals and gnarled tissue, healed into a disfiguring scar that had taken my voice, and nearly taken my life.

I barely remembered the attack: a large dark shape rushing at me from the shadows, then pain. Lots of pain. My mother told me I lay near death for days. No one thought I would survive, but I did.

Some believed it would be better if I hadn't. Even though I healed from the attack, the scars marked my face and my life. The boys used to chase me down the street, throwing things. I grew up learning to blend into the shadows. To move silently so I wouldn't draw attention to myself. Later, when my mother married my stepfather, I learned to cower and hide.

Her body is pretty enough, my stepfather had said. *Just put a bag over her head so you can stand it.*

Now my new owner tipped my head this way and that, studying the scar. He nodded, looking satisfied. "The mark of the wolf," he rasped.

A ripple went around the assembled men, and the other warriors pressed closer. The black haired man held me still, hefty arms around my body.

I wished I could ask what the blond warrior meant.

The men surrounded me, staring at my hideous scars.

My blond captor released my jaw and I ducked my head down again in shame. His large, rough hands caught my head again, and raised it, but this time he cupped my face.

I shut my eyes. I couldn't even cry out. This man now owned me. I'd resigned myself to living life with a disfigured face, unwanted and unloved, but I'd never thought I'd become a slave.

"Brenna," The command came in that rasping growl. "Look at me."

Somehow I obeyed and met the leader's steady gaze. Something in that golden glow mesmerized me, and I felt calmer.

"Do not be afraid." His throat worked for a moment, as if

he was trying to remember how to speak. "Is it true you cannot speak?"

I nodded.

"Can you read or write?"

I shook my head. This was the strangest conversation I'd had in my nineteen years.

He looked frustrated, exchanging glances with the warrior who held me.

A voice spoke at my ear, still rough and guttural, but a bit more clearly than before. "We would like to find a way to talk to ye." The speaker turned me to face him, and I flinched as he brought his hand up, but he only examined the scars as the blond had.

By the time he was done, all warriors but the blond had melted away. Dark hair touched my cheek and I winced, realizing there was a bruise on my face from when my step-father struck me.

The blond crowded closer, a sound rumbling in his great chest, not unlike a growl.

"Brenna," he said. "We will not hurt you. I swear it. No one will ever hurt you again."

The dark haired one took a few locks of my hair in his hand, gripping them lightly and raising them to his face. He breathed in my scent, then looked at me with glowing eyes and said in a clear voice.

"Ye belong to us now."

~

Sold to the Berserkers

When Brenna's father sells her to a band of passing warriors, her only thought is to survive. She doesn't expect to be claimed by the two fearsome warriors who lead the Berserker clan. Kept in captivity, she is coddled and cared for, treated more like a savior than a slave. Can captivity lead to love? And when she discovers the truth behind the myth of the fearsome warriors, can she accept her place as the Berserkers' true mate?

Author's Note: *Sold to the Berserkers is a standalone, short, MFM ménage romance starring two huge, dominant warriors who make it all about the woman. Read the whole best-selling Berserker saga to see what readers are raving about...*

~

THE BERSERKER SAGA

Sold to the Berserkers
Mated to the Berserkers
Bred by the Berserkers (FREE novella only available at
www.leesavino.com)
Taken by the Berserkers
Given to the Berserkers
Claimed by the Berserkers
Rescued by the Berserker - *free on all sites, including Wattpad*
Captured by the Berserkers
Kidnapped by the Berserkers
Bonded to the Berserkers